Amazing Grace

For our new sister
Kat... From Nancy
& Jim. Hope you
enjoy the story!
♡ . *jeloyle*

Amazing Grace

J. C. LAFLER

REDEMPTION
PRESS

Grace is the divine means by which God makes himself everything we need to utterly abound.

—2 Corinthians 9:8

ACKNOWLEDGMENT

In loving memory of my grandmother, Sarah B. Davis, who passed away many years ago. She would have loved this story! It is also dedicated to the women in my life, including my mom, LaJean Hewitt, and her best friend, Jackie Allen, who was like a second mom to me and always encouraged my love of books. And to the rest of the women—my sisters, my daughters, my granddaughters, my aunts, my nieces, my cousins, and my friends. Without all of your influence (and some of your names), this story would not have been the same. Thank you for your support. I hope you enjoy my story.

PROLOGUE

THE YOUNG MAN WALKED along the side of the road, carrying the heavy box. He stopped now and then to rest a bit and peeked sadly inside. Eventually, he trudged on. He saw a bus at the bus stop just ahead and hurried to the door. Pulling out the last of his money, he bought a ticket to the farthest point possible from where he had come. Nobody knew about what was in the box, so there was nobody to care or wonder where she had gone. His friend had left her and disappeared. She had talked about trying to find her a home, but now that was left for him to do. He couldn't take care of her. He was just another runaway himself. He had no job right now and never stayed in one place for long. But he couldn't just leave her. He had to find a place for her where someone would take care of her. And he had to do it tonight. There was only one bottle, a few instant formula packets, and a few diapers left. He had placed her nicest blanket under her, stuffed the few clothes that he could find around her in the box to help keep her warm and put an old knit hat on her head. He found an old blanket to wrap around the top of the box when he stopped to rest. It was January, and it was cold outside.

As the bus rumbled on and the baby slept, he dozed off. Several hours later, the bus came to a stop, and he was jerked awake. He picked up the box and headed down the bus steps. In the bus station, he went in the tiny restroom and locked the door. He sat the box on the floor and lifted her out. Placing her on the rickety changing table, he changed her diaper, hooking it like he had seen his friend do many times over the past couple of months. At least she would be dry. He refastened her sleeper and placed her back in the box. He held the bottle to her lips, but she didn't seem interested, so he put it back in the box beside her. He closed the box, picked it up, and headed outside. It was still cold and dark, but he could tell that nighttime was fading, and it would soon be dawn. He had to find a safe place for her before daylight.

He trudged along, looking for a church or school or somewhere he might leave her where she would be found and cared for. Just as he was starting to give up hope, a large house loomed up out of the darkness. Above the first floor windows was a sign that said "Heavenly Home for Girls." Perfect! He walked up the steps with a feeling of relief. He wrote a quick note and tucked it down in the bottom corner of the box, noticing she had fallen back asleep. He wrapped the old blanket around her, making sure she could still get air, and closed the box carefully to protect her as much as possible from the cold, noticing that the bushes around the front of the house would hide the box from view of the street. He placed the box up against the door, looked around to make sure nobody was watching, and walked away. As he went, he prayed silently, *Lord, please protect this child and help her to live a happy life. Amen.*

1

THEY FOUND HER OUTSIDE the school door one sunny January morning. She was bundled in a ragged old blanket inside a brown cardboard box with other miscellaneous clothing stuffed around her in an attempt to keep her warm. When Sarah went out to get the morning mail, she almost stumbled over the box. The baby's eyes were closed when Sarah pulled back the blanket, and she feared the baby might not be alive. Then the baby opened her dark-blue eyes and looked directly at her. Sarah snatched up the box and made her way back in the building, grabbing the mail so Mrs. Harper would not be mad, struggling to juggle the box and mail and get the door opened without dropping anything. The old woman would not be happy if her mail was late, and Sarah was already worrying about what Mrs. Harper would do with this new addition.

Once inside, there was no sign of Mrs. Harper, and her door was closed, so Sarah set the box down and placed the mail on the little table outside her office. She carefully carried the box into the huge room that Mrs. Harper insisted on calling the parlor and once again pulled back the blanket from the baby's face. The baby was quiet as Sarah pushed away the blanket and lifted her out of the box. Her little body seemed cool to the touch, although she was dressed in a very thick blanket sleeper in a faded shade of pink. Her head was covered by an old knitted hat, but her cheeks were rosy with the cold. Sarah gathered the baby close to her own body, trying to warm her up a bit. She heard a gurgling sound from the infant, so she lowered her back to her lap and spoke soothingly to her while removing the hat. Almost immediately, the baby responded to Sarah with the cutest smile Sarah had ever seen!

Sarah knew she would be in big trouble if she didn't tell Mrs. Harper about the baby, so she put her carefully back in the box and headed over to Mrs. Harper's office door. She knocked hesitantly. Mrs. Harper must have been on the phone because she told her to go away, or she would be sorry. Mrs. Harper hated to be interrupted by one of the girls when she was on the phone. Now what was she going to do?

Sarah heard little Lucy crying upstairs, so she hurried back into the parlor for the baby and headed up the stairs. When she got upstairs, she set the box on her bed and tended to Lucy, who had just woken up and was hungry. She went to their cupboard and pulled out the last package of biscuits and broke one in half and handed it to Lucy. Once Lucy was quiet, she called all the girls to come over and see her surprise. There were ten girls, including Sarah, all ranging in age from three to eleven. Sarah was the oldest at eleven, and Lucy was the youngest at three. Little Nora was four; Olivia was six; the twins, Sophie and Emma, were seven; Maddi and Gabbi were eight, and Katie and Kodi were nine. Sarah picked up the baby and held her gently on her lap. The girls looked at her in awe! They all started jostling one another to get closer, so Sarah quickly made room so all could see. The baby looked at them, blinked a couple of times, and promptly stuck her thumb in her mouth, which made them all giggle.

Katie asked to hold the baby, so Sarah handed her to Katie and cautioned her to be very careful with her. She scurried around, helping the younger girls get dressed, make their beds, and tidy up before Mrs. Harper came up to check things out. She would not be happy if things were not in order, and most of the time, she took it out on Sarah since she was the oldest. By the time everything was tidied up, the baby had started to fuss a bit. Sarah pulled open the box again, taking a better look at what was inside. Underneath the miscellaneous clothes that had been tucked around the infant, Sarah found a stack of disposable diapers and several packets of instant formula. She also found a bottle of milk! She quickly opened the bottle and smelled the milk, hoping it wasn't spoiled. It smelled okay, so she screwed the cap back on and walked over to the baby to see if that would quiet her. The milk was cold, but the baby sucked on the bottle happily, so Sarah settled her with Kodi, who was dressed and had finished tidying her area. Then she hurried to help Katie do the same.

Once the baby had finished her bottle, she started to cry. Sarah hurried to Kodi and took the baby, hoping to quiet her before Mrs. Harper heard her. She could tell the little one had a soggy diaper, so she put her carefully on her bed and pulled out a diaper to change her. She seemed to know instinctively how to take care of her. The baby continued to whimper until the wet diaper had been replaced with a dry one. As Sarah bent to pick up the baby, who had stopped crying, Mrs. Harper appeared at the top of the stairs. "What is going on up here!" she shouted.

Mrs. Harper had black hair that she wore in a very tight bun. She wore a dark skirt and a white blouse every day, and her blouse tended to come untucked a bit when she moved around or bent over. She seemed horribly mean to the girls. She rarely had a kind word for anyone, and she yelled a *lot*! Her voice was sort of screechy-sounding when she yelled, almost fake-sounding, which made the girls nervous. She was always threatening to throw them out if she didn't like what they were doing, and she once told Sarah she would lock them in the basement if they didn't keep things picked up. Luckily for them, she was also very forgetful. Often she forgot what she was doing and didn't make good on her threats. Some days she stayed in her office, and the girls didn't see her all day. Those were the good days.

When she saw Sarah holding the baby, she marched over to her. "Where did you get that baby!" she screamed in her face.

"I found her on the doorstep this morning when I went to get the mail," Sarah replied. "Isn't she adorable?"

"Adorable!" Mrs. Harper screeched. "Do you know what it costs to take care of a baby these days? Put her back immediately!"

"But Mrs. Harper," Sarah argued, "it's so cold outside. We have to call someone. Please."

"Fine," Mrs. Harper tried to snarl, but it came out a bit shaky. "I'll call Child Protective Services, and they can come and get the brat!" She marched off down the stairs, but Sarah saw her look back over her shoulder with a worried look on her face.

"Don't worry, girls!" Sarah said as she noticed that the little ones were upset at Mrs. Harper's screaming. "Maybe she'll forget. Let's pretend this is our new baby sister, and Mama has left her in our care while she gets us groceries. Who wants to hold her first? Be careful now and make sure everyone gets to hold her for a bit. Katie and Kodi, can you help the little ones?"

As Sarah kept a close eye on her little brood, she heard a sweet giggle from Nora as the baby looked at her and smiled. She went about her normal cleaning, checking their bathroom, straightening towels, and picking up a stray article of clothing here and there. This was a nice change for the girls, and the baby seemed content going from one to the other amid coos and giggles. If only it could always be like this. But Sarah knew from past experience that the element of unpleasantness could creep back and surround them at a moment's notice.

2

SARAH LOOKED AROUND THEIR "home" and wondered how she had come to this. Four years ago, she had lost the most wonderful parents a girl could ask for. They had gone out for dinner one night and never returned. Icy roads had caused them to slide off the road and roll down a steep hill, landing in the water at the bottom. Since both of her parents were only children and their parents had already passed, there was no one to reach out to for Sarah to live with. Child Protective Services (CPS) had tried to find her foster parents, but there was no one available at the time. Mrs. Harper had just opened her school, so they contacted her, and she was sent to Mrs. Harper's Heavenly Home for Girls. Unfortunately, there was nothing very heavenly about the place. Mrs. Harper had twin stepdaughters (Sophie and Emma) who were only three at the time, and it was soon clear that Sarah was going to be expected to take care of them. Their mother had died when they were born, and their father had married Mrs. Harper the year they turned two. Unfortunately, he had died unexpectedly a year later from a rare form of cancer. Mrs. Harper was bitter about his death and was no longer happy about having to raise two little girls. Sarah felt bad for the little girls, and in spite of her own sorrow over losing her parents, she lavished all the love she had on them. In return, they adored her! They were very pretty little girls, with dark-auburn hair and big blue eyes. And they were easy to tell apart because while Emma's hair was completely straight, Sophie's hair was nothing but curls!

Mrs. Harper was critical and mean to all of them and was only friendly when CPS visited, or adoptive parents were visiting, which was rare. She promised every visitor that the girls loved the school and were a joy to have around. What a joke! They barely had enough to eat and took care of themselves. Sarah knew that Mrs. Harper got more money with each girl who came to live at the school, but she complained constantly about how much she had to spend on them. Sarah gave her a list of things they needed, but often she didn't get it all or didn't get enough for everyone. She wanted all the money for herself. With the addition of Lucy recently, they didn't even have enough beds. They lived upstairs in one large room that had four sets of cheap bunk beds, a trundle bed, a tiny bathroom, and a table and chairs. One of the bottom bunks didn't have a mattress and was broken, so she was forced to put Lucy in with Nora, putting one at each end of the trundle bed that pulled out from under her bed. It worked for now as they were both so small, but Sarah didn't know what would happen if they all stayed. When she mentioned to Mrs. Harper that they needed to fix the broken bed, she brushed it off, saying maybe one of them would get adopted soon, or CPS would find foster parents. Sarah knew Lucy and Nora had the best chance of getting a family at their ages, but she also knew that Mrs. Harper did absolutely nothing to enhance their chances. She only seemed interested in the check that came every month to cover each girl's expenses. And Sarah thought she worked really hard at not caring about any of them.

Mrs. Harper's answer to schooling was to hire a part-time teacher who came in three times a week to work with them for the afternoon. In spite of the fact that "complete and age-appropriate schooling" was supposed to be provided at the home, the truth was that there were too many girls, and the education the girls got from the part-time teacher and what Sarah was able to provide was definitely *not* complete and age-appropriate schooling. She didn't have much to work with, but the teacher who came to the school was really nice and provided them with paper and pencils and books, in addition to the skimpy supplies that Mrs. Harper bought them. They had a few videos that were old, and they were allowed to watch educational programs on the rickety TV downstairs at certain times of the day. There were a few raggedy storybooks for pleasure, but mostly Sarah relied on a big leather-bound Bible that she had brought with her when she first arrived. It was the one familiar thing Sarah had when she first got to the school, and she kept it hidden in her drawer. It was a child's Bible, but she cherished it. She read to the girls from it at night, and it was something they all looked forward to. The Bible had her parents' names in it and a family picture of them when Sarah was born. It was all she had left of her family.

Sarah was a wonderful reader and, thankfully, was very advanced for her age when she got to the school. Her parents had doted on her, especially when she showed an aptitude to read early on and had taken her to the best schools available. They also went to church regularly and taught her about God and faith. She had loved her pastor and his wife, and their church had lots of fun events and Sunday school classes for the children. Sarah loved to write poems, and she had a poem published in her Sunday school paper when she was only six years old! But that was a thing of the past now, and her memories of it were fading away.

Mrs. Harper had picked up quickly on the fact that Sarah was big enough and smart enough to take care of the others and had quickly begun to expect her to make sure all the chores were done and lessons were completed too. While she bragged to visitors and CPS that she provided educational classes and schooling for all of "her" girls, it was Sarah who made sure they watched the outdated videos and taught the little ones their letters and numbers and colors, with the help of Miss Debbie, the part-time teacher.

With the addition of Katie and Kodi a year ago, her load had gotten slightly easier when it came to watching over the little ones, but there was also the added worry of two extra girls to be responsible for. Katie and Kodi were cousins, but Katie could be a real stinker at times! One time, she snitched a couple of cookies from Mrs. Harper's desk when she saw them from the open doorway, and Mrs. Harper made them all go without dinner when she discovered them missing and no one would confess to taking them. Katie had broken the cookies into little pieces and shared them with the girls, who all kept her secret. Kodi, with her dark-brown skin and eyes, was a contrast to Katie in every way. Her quiet demeanor complemented and calmed Katie, who was often a bit hyper. Katie's coloring was as light as Kodi's was dark, with almost porcelain skin and very light-brown hair. And while Kodi kept her dark hair brushed and tidy, Katie's hair was always a tangled mess. Sarah knew they had been removed from an extremely rough environment, and both girls seemed happy to be somewhere more stable. But Sarah once overheard Katie and Kodi talking about running away if Mrs. Harper got any worse. She prayed that would not happen. Sarah loved all the girls, but it was a tough job being responsible for all of them and making sure they had what they needed. And Mrs. Harper's sharpness was unsettling for all of them. Sometimes she just wished she could go back to being a kid herself.

Now Sarah had a baby to worry about. What would Mrs. Harper do about her? Would CPS come and take her away? Where had she come from? Sarah glanced over and noticed that little Maddi had sung the baby to sleep. Maddi had a soft, pretty voice and was always singing! Sarah walked over and gently picked up the baby and laid her on the bed that she slept in. She put her pillow in front of the baby in case she woke up or wiggled in her sleep and gathered all the girls over to their "kitchen area" to have breakfast.

Their kitchen area consisted of a large cupboard at the other end of their room with a small counter beside it and a long table with mismatched chairs. There was a small refrigerator in the bottom of the cupboard with a microwave on the shelf above it. There was another shelf above the microwave for dishes. Sarah used a little step stool to reach the dishes and got out the ten plastic bowls that they used for cereal and the ten spoons that stood in a cup beside them. She set them on the table, and the girls quickly passed them around. She stepped down and picked up the box of presweetened wheat puffs, and each girl waited while she poured some in their bowl. She opened the tiny fridge and took out one of the containers of milk and again went around the table. She threw the empty milk container away and sat down with the girls. In unison, the girls all folded their hands together, and Sarah picked one of the girls to lead the prayer: "God is good. God is great. Let us thank Him for our food. Amen." Then all ten girls gobbled up their cereal. Afterward, they decided whose turn it was to clean the dishes in the bathroom sink and dry them. When they finished, Sarah would place them back on the shelf for the next meal.

Sarah settled each of the girls with a lesson to work on, giving the little ones crayons and paper, and went back to the box the baby had come in. She took out one of the packets of milk, cleaned the bottle that the baby had finished earlier, and set to work mixing the formula for another bottle. Once she added the water and stirred it thoroughly, she placed the bottle in the refrigerator for the baby's next meal. She sat down and sorted through the articles of clothing that had been stuffed around the baby with everything else. There were a couple of sleepers, five more diapers, and five more packets of formula. There was a soft blanket on the bottom, much nicer than the raggedy, heavier blanket on top that had covered the baby in the box. Someone had cared enough about the baby to make sure the basics were with her.

Sarah took the blanket out and folded it carefully to use for the baby. She hoped someone kind would take the baby if they couldn't keep her. And she hoped whoever had given her up was okay too. As Sarah was putting everything back in the box, she noticed something white in the corner. It was a tiny folded note! When she opened the note, it said simply, "This baby needs a home, but I cannot keep her. Please take care of her." What did it mean? Should she tell Mrs. Harper? Before she could decide, she heard Mrs. Harper coming up the stairs. Making a split-second decision, she ran over to her drawer and stuck the note in her Bible. She returned quickly to the table by the children.

3

SARAH COULD SEE INSTANTLY that Mrs. Harper was not happy. She marched right over to Sarah as if it were her fault. "Well, young lady, we are stuck with that baby until I can get CPS to call me back and they can get over here and get it. I certainly hope you know what to do until then. I have not had to deal with a baby for years, and I have no idea what to do."

"It's no problem, Mrs. Harper," Sarah replied. "She doesn't need much, and I found some diapers and milk mix in the box. I already made her another bottle, and there is enough for more bottles if she is still hungry. I can make sure she has a dry diaper, and I think that is all she will need for now."

"Fine, you take care of her then since you seem to know all about it!" Mrs. Harper snapped. And with that, she marched right back down the stairs without another word. She didn't even remember to do her daily inspection, and the girls breathed easier as soon as she was gone. Of course, no one was aware that Mrs. Harper bowed her head and cried when she returned to her office, worried that, once again, fate had dealt her a low blow. She didn't want to deal with somebody else's baby, and she needed Sarah to take care of the other girls. Why did these things keep happening to her?

The baby slept for several hours, and the girls went about their day. Lunch was microwaved soup and crackers, and afterward, it was time to go downstairs to watch an educational program on the television. Sarah took the bottle out of the refrigerator and set it in a bowl of hot water to take the chill off (she had seen her mom do this once when she cared for the neighbor's baby), then picked up the baby as she started to fuss behind the pillow. She woke up a bit startled, so Sarah held her close and patted her back. It seemed to soothe her, and soon her big bright eyes were looking around again. Sarah noticed the big clock on the wall and saw that the little hand was almost on the one, which meant their program was about to start on the Discovery Channel. She asked Kodi to take the lead and line the girls up to go downstairs. They went in single file, very quietly, because Mrs. Harper did not want to hear them pounding down the stairs. She really did not want to hear them at all! Sarah got the bottle of milk and a paper towel to wrap around it and hurried after the girls. The girls quietly gathered on the floor near the TV, and Katie expertly turned it on to the right channel just as the program started. Today's show was about the planets, and the girls were quickly engrossed in hearing about the heavens and stars and all the different sizes and colors of the planets.

Sarah sat with the baby near the girls, leaning her back on the sofa and watching the infant as she quickly gobbled down the bottle of milk. Once finished, she seemed content to sit on Sarah's lap and watch the TV with the rest of them. Sarah enjoyed these shows as much as the girls did, and it was one of the only ways she could get new information to share with the others. Usually, she wrote down some of the main points to use in answering the inevitable questions that came afterward, but today she just sat there and listened, gently swaying with the baby just a bit to keep her happy. The baby was not very big, but she was very alert and aware of what was going on around her. Sarah had noticed that it said three months on the tag in one of the sleepers upstairs, so she guessed her to be about that old. She couldn't help but think about the note, and suddenly she knew what they could call this baby!

That night, when Sarah got out her book, she decided to share the story of Noah and the ark. The girls eagerly got ready and climbed into their designated beds. Sarah shared how God had come to Noah and asked him to build the ark, bringing in pairs of animals of every kind. The girls loved this part and tried to make the noises of all the animals, until Sarah hushed them in fear of Mrs. Harper hearing them and making them turn out lights early. When Sarah finished the story, she pointed out a particular verse in the Bible. "Genesis 6:8 says, 'But Noah found grace in the eyes of the Lord.' Do you all know what that means?" When she saw negative nods from the girls, she explained that Noah's faith in God's promises saved him and his family from death in the flood. It was the gift of God's grace that made it all possible. Looking around, she started seeing the older girls nodding their understanding. At that point, she decided to make her suggestion. "What if this baby was put here for a reason?" Sarah went on, "I don't know how long she will be here, but we need to call her something other than the baby. What do you all think about calling her *Grace?*" The girls all nodded excitedly. "It will be our little secret, so let's not mention it to Mrs. Harper, okay?"

Once again, the girls all agreed, and little Nora said solemnly, "She will be our little gift from God!" She leaned up to the baby and called her by name. "Hello, Grace," she said to the baby, placing her hands on either side of her face. "Do you like your new name?" The baby looked back at Nora, and suddenly she smiled.

"Well, that settles it," Sarah said. "Grace it is!" She laid the baby back in the box that she had arranged, tucking the soft blanket on top around her, and went to each girl's bed to say prayers. She ended up with Nora and Lucy, listening patiently while they blessed everyone and everything they could think of. Sarah pushed Nora's baby-fine blonde hair out of her eyes as she tucked her in with Lucy. When everyone was finally settled, Sarah turned off the big light, leaving the night-light on in the bathroom, and climbed into her own bed. The baby was asleep, so Sarah curled herself around her as best she could and tried to get some sleep herself. She didn't hear Mrs. Harper sneak quietly up the stairs later that night to stand over the sleeping baby. She touched the softness of the baby's cheek, looked around sadly at the rest of the sleeping children, and disappeared as quietly as she had come.

The next morning, the children awoke to a ruckus! They could hear Mrs. Harper yelling all the way up the stairs from her office. "You have to take the baby today!" she yelled in her screechy, shaky voice. "We don't have anything to take care of a baby here! We don't even know where it came from!" There was a bit of silence while someone on the other end of the phone was talking. "She needs a crib and diapers and formula," Mrs. Harper continued. "I don't have all of that here, and I'm not buying it! Why would I want to take care of a baby! It's ridiculous!"

Sarah encouraged the girls to use the bathroom, get dressed, and make up beds as she listened to see if Mrs. Harper would say more. She juggled little Grace on one hip while she drew hot water in a bowl to warm the bottle she had made the day before. All of a sudden, they all heard Mrs. Harper exclaim, "Fine. I'll keep her until then, but you had better bring what she needs today! And don't forget the check. I want a month in advance!" With that, she threw her phone down on her desk. At that point, she must have realized her office door was open, and they heard a loud slam! as she pushed it shut.

Sarah asked Kodi to feed the baby and settled them on her bed before getting the others breakfast. Today was Wednesday, so Miss Debbie would be coming in the afternoon for classes. Once she had everyone's breakfast poured, Sarah took the baby from Kodi so she could go and eat hers and sat with the baby as she finished her bottle. She nibbled on a bowl of dry cereal herself, knowing that their milk was getting low. She needed to give Mrs. Harper a list today, which she dreaded. And now she would have to add things for the baby.

4

AFTER BREAKFAST WAS CLEANED up and dishes put away, she settled the girls at the table to finish their papers in preparation for Miss Debbie. She carefully changed Grace's diaper and put her into one of the other sleepers, putting the soiled one in the hamper for Thursday's laundry. Grace seemed content, and Sarah gave her a little squeeze and a tickle, which brought out her happy smile. All of a sudden, Mrs. Harper was pounding up the stairs and into their room. She was out of breath, but she hurriedly made her way around the room, looking for anything out of place. Instead of her usual critical comments, today she was in a hurry. She actually half smiled at the girls and told them what a good job they were doing with their papers. Her demeanor was quickly explained as two men followed her up the stairs, carrying various pieces of baby furniture and supplies.

There was a crib and mattress, high chair, and even a changing table! The girls looked on in awe as the men placed the crib and changing table against the wall near the trundle bed and put the high chair near the table. One of the men opened the cupboard under the changing table and showed Mrs. Harper a variety of baby items. There were several sizes of disposable diapers, sleepers, bibs, blankets, etc., for the baby. There was a small tub on the bottom shelf that was full of baby shampoo and wash, baby lotion, diaper ointment, cotton swabs, thermometer, and all the things necessary for a baby. Sarah hurried over with the baby, hardly believing her eyes and thanking the men over and over again. One of the men noticed the broken bottom bunk and asked Mrs. Harper if she would like him to fix it. She was all about taking advantage of these men, so she agreed immediately, and one of the men left to get what he needed from his truck.

In the meantime, Mrs. Rogers, the tired old lady from CPS, finally made it up the stairs with several bags of her own. She walked over to the counter behind the table to show Mrs. Harper the rest of the stuff she had brought. The first bag held several canisters of baby formula. Mrs. Rogers showed Mrs. Harper that it was for babies three to six months and was the kind that you just added water to (as if Mrs. Harper cared, Sarah thought). Next, Mrs. Rogers pulled out a variety of early baby food jars that could be used when the baby was ready. She also had several bottles of baby water, vitamins, and a box of teething biscuits that were baby-friendly. Mrs. Harper thanked her and nodded as if she understood everything.

Finally, Mrs. Rogers opened the last couple of bags that had some treats for the girls. She explained that Kellogg's, a nearby cereal company, had donated breakfast tarts, cereal, fruit snacks, and cookies for the school, and she pulled out more treats than the girls had ever had. The girls were so excited they started talking about what they wanted and only quieted when Mrs. Harper turned and glared at them, unseen by Mrs. Rogers. Not realizing the true situation, Mrs. Rogers opened a large bag of animal cookies and started passing them around to all the girls. Mrs. Harper was forced to go along with it, but Sarah could see the terseness of her smile and knew she wasn't pleased. Still, she couldn't help but hope that Mrs. Harper would let them keep at least some of them. The last bag was full of macaroni-and-cheese dinners, soups, crackers, and several multipacks of pudding and fruits. Sarah almost cried. She was so happy to see all the food. She had noticed that Mrs. Rogers had already placed a container of milk and some butter in the refrigerator, frowning a bit at the lack of food inside. She carefully folded the bags and stacked them neatly, saying she would be happy to stop by next week and see if there was anything else they needed.

The man came back upstairs with his tool bag and was able to put new screws in the frame and fix the part of the mattress support that was broken. He jiggled the other frames and took a minute to tighten up any loose bolts or screws in them as well. He spoke to Mrs. Rogers and

Mrs. Harper, asking if they used the other bunk and were interested in a mattress for it. He had one in his garage that he could drop off if they wanted it. Sarah's mind was racing! Suddenly they had extra food and maybe an extra bed! Mrs. Harper nodded her head again, telling him it would be wonderful, if he didn't mind dropping it off. The man smiled at the girls, tweaked little Lucy's pigtail, and said it would be his pleasure. As the adults headed toward the stairs, Mrs. Harper trailed behind, waiting until they were out of sight before turning back to the girls, pointing at the food and Sarah, and mouthing, "I'll be right back. Don't touch anything!"

Sarah heard them talking and saying their good-byes, so she handed baby Grace to Katie, picked up a packet of cookies and one of the fruit snacks, and rushed over to hide them in her drawer at the end of the trundle. She rushed back and took the baby and stood innocently chatting with the girls when Mrs. Harper returned.

Mrs. Harper walked quickly over to the counter and began sorting through the food. "This is way too much food to keep up here, and too much sugar for kids," she mumbled. "I'll take some of it down to the kitchen." She sorted out the chocolate chip cookies, her favorite cereal, and even took some of the breakfast tarts and fruit snacks. "I expect you won't need any groceries this week, so don't bother with a list!" she snapped as she headed down the stairs with her goodies.

Lucy started to cry, and Nora joined right in. "She took our goodies. She's bad!" Olivia said out of the blue. Olivia was a quiet little girl with olive skin, long dark hair, and slightly slanted eyes. She rarely had anything bad to say and was usually very kind.

"It's okay," Sarah encouraged the girls, rubbing little Lucy's back and patting Nora's shoulder. "We still have plenty, and you all got cookies too!" She handed Grace to Katie so she could put away their "groceries." There were so many items it filled the shelves in the cupboard, so she put the puddings and fruit in the refrigerator. She went over and found a sheet in the changing table for the crib and set about fixing it up. There were even a couple of toys with rubber rings and crinkly paper and a little ring of animals that attached to the crib and played music. She called Katie over and placed Grace in the crib. Grace's eyes were bright as she watched the little animals go round and round to the music. The girls all gathered around the crib in joy at the sight.

5

THE REST OF THE day passed quickly, and Miss Debbie was surprised to meet little Grace when she arrived in the afternoon. She secretly worried about the extra work that meant for Sarah but fell in love with Grace immediately, even holding her so Sarah could actually do some reading and writing of her own. Over the last couple of years, Miss Debbie had learned quite a bit about Sarah. She knew the girl was gifted academically and tried to give her lessons that would challenge her gift. She also knew that Sarah worked hard and got little appreciation in return from Mrs. Harper. Sarah's birthday was at the end of the month, and she was hoping to do something very special for the girl. She would have to get Mrs. Harper's approval, but she would threaten her if she had to. What made her so hateful anyway?

Mrs. Harper was an old friend of Miss Debbie's and definitely took advantage of the fact. She paid her next to nothing to teach these girls, and she knew it. Miss Debbie didn't think she would take a chance of losing that since she would have a very hard time finding someone else to do it for so little money. Lucky for Miss Debbie, money was not a problem for her. She had lived alone all her life, saved well, and had very little to spend money on. She was just as happy to care for the girls as they were to have her. These girls were delightful, and she wished she had room to adopt them all herself! Alas, her house was barely big enough for her and an occasional guest. There just hadn't been a reason to buy something bigger over the years, and it was in a very old, quiet area. Not a place for children.

Miss Debbie laid Grace gently in the crib as she had fallen asleep. She walked around the table, looking over the girls' work and adding a comment here and there. The girls were doing pretty well, for the most part. Each of them had their strong and weak points, but Miss Debbie could tell that Sarah was encouraging them and doing a great job answering their questions in her absence. She pulled Sarah aside and asked if there was anything she needed or if she had any questions. Sarah assured her the girls were doing well, asking only about some flash cards in multiplication for Kodi. Kodi was doing a great job in math but wanted to learn multiplication. Miss Debbie told her she had several sets of different flash cards that she would bring on Friday. Then she asked Sarah how *she* was doing. Sarah avoided the question, although Miss Debbie could see something was troubling her.

"Well, if you think of anything, write it down and give it to me on Friday," Miss Debbie said. "You are doing a *great* job with these girls, Sarah! They are so lucky to have you!" With that, she popped a gummy Life Saver into each girl's mouth in turn and said her good-byes, telling them all she would see them on Friday.

Just after Miss Debbie left, the man came back bringing the mattress for the lower bunk and a large bag. Mrs. Harper marched up the stairs behind him, oohing and ahhing as if he was the most wonderful person in the world. And truly, the girls thought he was! He put the mattress on the bottom bunk, and Sarah could see that it was very nice. He reached into the bag and brought out sheets for the bed as well and a whole pile of blankets. Each girl had only one cover to use on their bed, and some of them were quite thin, so they were very excited to have the extra blankets. The man said his name was Mr. Frank and made a fuss about figuring out which blanket each girl would like. Looking at their neatly made-up beds, he suggested they keep it right at the end of their beds. The girls cuddled their new blankets (many of them looked brand-new to Sarah) and exclaimed about how soft they were. Noticing that Sarah had the thinnest blanket of all, Mr. Frank handed her a soft, fluffy blanket in a bright, pretty blue. "To match your eyes," he said with a wink.

Sarah didn't know what to say, so she just thanked him again and quickly folded up her blanket and placed it at the foot of her bed. Finally, Mr. Frank turned to Mrs. Harper, smiling, and told her he would stop back by in a week or so to see how the bed was holding out. He told her to let him know anytime they needed something fixed. He was a handyman and was out and about a lot and didn't mind stopping by now and then. He told the girls good-bye and headed toward the stairs with Mrs. Harper right on his heels, gushing about his kindness.

Sarah looked at all the girls holding their new blankets lovingly. At first, she worried that Mrs. Harper might take them; but since the man promised to come back now and then, Sarah didn't think she would dare to take them and have him asking questions. She focused on the blessings they had received instead. Now Nora could have her very own bed, leaving just little Lucy to sleep in the small trundle that pulled out from under Sarah's bed. And all the girls would be warmer with their new blankets. She didn't even have to worry about baby Grace, now that she had a crib to sleep in. It had been a great day indeed!

That night, after Grace was sleeping, Sarah read to the girls about the Psalms of David. She explained to them all that no matter what David was facing in good times and bad times, he always poured out gratitude to God and focused on the truth of God's goodness. "Psalm 9:1 says, 'I will give thanks to the Lord with my whole heart; I will recount all of your wonderful deeds.' And Psalm 100:1–5 says, 'Make a joyful noise to the Lord, all the earth! Serve the Lord with gladness! Come into His presence with singing! Know that the Lord, He is God! It is He who made us, and we are His; we are His people, and the sheep of His pasture. Enter His gates with thanksgiving, and His courts with praise! Give thanks to Him, bless His name! For the Lord is good; His steadfast love endures forever, and His faithfulness to all generations.' I think this means that if we learn to simply be grateful for the things we have every day and have a loving heart, God will bless us and provide for us," Sarah shared.

"Are you saying that if people are mean and selfish, we should still feel loving toward them?" Olivia asked quietly.

Sarah knew she was thinking about what happened earlier when Mrs. Harper took their new goodies. "Olivia, I think the answer is yes. We should still try to be loving ourselves and give thanks to God for all that we have. When someone does something mean, acting mean back doesn't help the situation. And we don't want to act like the mean person we dislike, do we?"

Olivia solemnly shook her head no.

"Okay, girls, I think we have a lot to be extra thankful for today, don't you?" As the girls nodded and hugged their new blankets even closer, Sarah suggested they sing a nighttime song before prayers.

"I'll start, I'll start!" Maddi said, and she began singing. "Jesus loves the little children, all the children in the world, red and yellow, black and white, they are precious in his sight. Jesus loves the little children of the world."

Soon all the girls joined in quietly and sang the song. Looking around the beds at each of them, Sarah thought it was a very appropriate song. As she lay in her own bed after the lights were out, Sarah said her prayers as well, asking God for guidance and protection for all of them.

6

THE NEXT DAY, IT snowed and snowed, and the girls watched it out the windows in the parlor that afternoon as they listened to their Thursday program on the television. They thought it would be fun to play outside in the snow, but of course, they did not have the proper clothing. Mrs. Harper only let them play out in the fenced backyard when the weather was nicer. During the winter, they were forced to stay in the house, although Sarah would sometimes pick one of them to go with her to get the mail each day. Besides, today was laundry day. This meant extra work for all of them as laundry was carried down to the laundry room, washed, dried, and carried back upstairs to be folded and put in their drawers or the boxes under their beds. As they made their way back upstairs after the program, Mrs. Harper stuck her head out of the office to tell them Miss Debbie would not be there tomorrow because of the weather and snowy roads. The girls trudged up the stairs even sadder, knowing that they would not get to see Miss Debbie, which also meant no treats or kind words!

To cheer them up a bit, Sarah helped the girls create snowflakes out of white paper. She took the ball of string and the Scotch tape that Miss Debbie had added to their school supplies during one of their lessons and began to hang the snowflakes around the room. Soon the girls were admiring all the beautiful snowflakes they had created. They were so busy with their snowflakes that no one noticed how quiet Sarah was. Sarah was thinking about the news alert on the television that she had noticed as the girls were heading back upstairs, and she was walking over to turn it off. Someone was reporting a missing child, which made her sad and made her wonder again about who had left the baby on their doorstep. At least they were all together and inside out of the weather.

The weekend passed slowly for Sarah, and the girls were restless and a bit cranky at times. Even baby Grace seemed a little fussier than usual, so Sarah decided to give each of the girls a period of time to watch over Grace and keep her happy. Katie and Kodi paired up with Lucy and Nora, and even little Lucy had fun holding different toys for the baby and making funny faces at her to make her laugh. Soon it became a bit of a contest to see who could make Grace smile or laugh the most. Katie and Kodi had also become experts at changing her, so it gave Sarah a bit of time to work on her own lessons.

The last day in January was Sarah's twelfth birthday, and she was beginning to worry about all the things she was missing and wondering about the "stuff" that she had questions about. Other than Miss Debbie, she really didn't have anyone to teach her about life and what to expect. She wondered if this was going to be her life forever. As much as she loved the girls, she longed for a life of her own too. She knew she would need more education as she got older and hoped eventually to be able to plan for a career and maybe even life outside the school. She wasn't even sure how long CPS would continue to pay for her to reside at the home, but she didn't feel comfortable asking Mrs. Harper. She knew that Mrs. Harper needed her to look after the girls, and the girls would be afraid and sad without her. She couldn't just leave them and only think of herself!

At that point, she pushed her thoughts to the side, knowing there was no easy answer. She knew from reading every page of her Bible over and over that the best thing she could do was to pray and have faith that God would lead her to the right place at the right time. She still remembered praying with her parents and was ever thankful for what they had taught her in their short years together. It was what had gotten Sarah through the lonely nights since, that and the other girls' needs. She had poured herself into caring for them with all her heart. She reminded herself to read the passage in Proverbs about needing to know God's will in your life (Proverbs 3:1–6). It would help her to remember to trust Him rather than trying to understand everything that was happening. Right now, these girls needed her, and she knew this was where she should be.

Sarah put her paper and pencil away, folded her note for Miss Debbie about CPS, and got out her Bible to pick a story for the girls. She watched as Gabbi pushed her long curly hair away from baby Gracie's fingers. Gabbi's hair was past her waist and fell in soft fuzzy curls, which gave her fits at times but was extraordinarily beautiful. She had soft brown skin and big brown eyes that often sparkled with mischief. She had been extremely quiet and withdrawn when she first came to the school. Sarah wasn't sure about her background but had pieced together a couple of things from talking with Miss Debbie and to Gabbi herself. It seemed her father was in prison, and her mother had a new boyfriend who thought Gabbi belonged in a boarding school. At first, they picked her up for occasional weekends; but eventually, she just stayed at the school full-time. Sarah guessed that her mom's boyfriend didn't care for the color of Gabbi's skin and had decided she didn't "fit" well in their new family.

It was difficult for Gabbi at first, and she cried for her mother and begged Sarah to call her, especially at night. But when Maddi arrived, the two girls bonded together almost instantly, consoling each other and sharing their stories. Being the same age, they had something in common right from the start, so it was no wonder they reached for each other. The two of them were close friends now and loved doing things together. They had decided to combine their time for watching Grace and do it together. Maddi peeked over Gabbi's shoulder as she held the baby, playing peekaboo with Grace and making her giggle harder each time she did it! They were so silly! Earlier, they had been singing a song that Maddi created. It was a sort of "rap" for the baby and had all the girls laughing and clapping until Sarah hushed them so Mrs. Harper wouldn't come upstairs to shush them herself.

Maddi had dark-brown hair and eyes and was lean and athletic. Like Sarah, Maddi had lost her parents to a car accident, but she had been living with her grandma for the past couple of years. When her grandmother became ill and needed surgery, Mrs. Harper's Heavenly Home for Girls seemed like the perfect answer, especially short-term. Unfortunately, the surgery did not go well, and Maddi's grandmother passed away. Still, after a few rough weeks, Maddi adjusted to Sarah and was also able to count on Gabbi for understanding. Maddi's grandmother had left instructions and money for Maddi to stay at the Heavenly Home for Girls. She was a welcome addition to their little family in a lot of ways. She was the cheerleader in their group, always trying to cheer the girls up when there was a problem. She was also their resident hairdresser, always fixing one of the girls' hairs in a ponytail or braids or bun. She loved trying different styles on them, and even Sarah enjoyed it when Maddi brushed and braided her hair.

Little Gracie giggled out loud, and Sarah smiled. The baby had brought a new and much-needed air of happiness to the group as well. It gave them all a sense of accomplishment to know they were caring for another individual who didn't seem to have a family either. It helped the younger girls to realize they needed to give up their babyish ways because now they had a real baby in their midst. Little Lucy had not had an accident since Grace had been with them. She didn't want to wet her pants like the baby did because she was a big girl now and Grace was the baby. When she told Sarah this very seriously one day, it was all Sarah could do to keep from laughing. But so far, Lucy had been true to her word and had not had one accident. She walked around telling all the girls what a big girl she was when she woke up dry every morning. Lucy had wispy reddish-blonde curls that bounced as she walked, and with her green eyes wide and serious, she was hard to resist. She looked nothing like the scared little girl who had first come to live with them.

7

THE REST OF JANUARY passed without any more surprises, until the very last week. When Miss Debbie came to see the girls the last Wednesday in January, she told them she had a big surprise for them all. She went on to explain that since Friday was Miss Sarah's birthday, she had gotten permission from Mrs. Harper to take them all out to supper, even baby Grace! The girls all looked around at one another in disbelief! They had *never* gotten to do anything like this. They all started asking questions at once. "Who's taking us?" "How will we all fit?" "How do we pay for it?" "What about a seat for Grace?" The questions just poured out before Miss Debbie could even answer the first one. Finally, Miss Debbie raised her hand, motioning for all of them to be quiet. "I have it all arranged," she said. "My sisters, Becky and Jill, and each of their teenage granddaughters are going to come with us. We will use my church's bus to transport you all, and I have also borrowed car seats for those who need them. We will have our regular lesson from one to three o'clock, then they will arrive afterward to pick us up. My church is preparing a special dinner for you all, with ice cream and cake for dessert, so of course, no money is required. Who wants to go?" A loud chorus of, "I do! I do!" followed, causing Miss Debbie to once again raise her hand, signaling for quiet. "Okay, let's finish our lessons today. On Friday, I will bring extra supplies so each of you can think about what kind of card you want to make for Miss Sarah."

As the girls settled into their lessons, Sarah walked over to Miss Debbie with tears in her eyes and gave her a hug. "Thank you so much!" she exclaimed. "I haven't had a birthday party in so long! And this will be the girls' first party since we have all been together!" Miss Debbie smiled at Sarah and said it was about time they all had a party then!

After Miss Debbie left, the girls chattered on and on about the party. Sarah had given Miss Debbie another big hug to show her thanks when she handed her the note about CPS. She could hardly wait till Friday herself! Supper outside of the home and ice cream and cake sounded wonderful! Even little Grace seemed to sense the air of excitement as she cooed and smiled at the girls after dinner that night. Sarah reminded all the girls to pray for Miss Debbie and give thanks to God for all their blessings. Tucking Nora into her new bed on the repaired bunk, Sarah marveled at all that had happened in this first month of the year. She could only hope and pray that the rest of the year wouldn't be a letdown after such a wonderful January! She knew God was watching over them and answering her prayers for guidance.

Friday afternoon, lessons were filled with excitement! Miss Debbie kept the girls busy with cards for Sarah, and Sarah used the time to give Grace a bottle and a fresh bath. She picked out a cute outfit that she found in the cupboard under the changing table and put together an extra diaper and bottle to take with them in case they needed it. She was as excited as the girls when the time came for the church bus to arrive. When the bus arrived, Miss Debbie led the way downstairs, patting the scowling Mrs. Harper's shoulder and telling her not to be such a sour puss! The girls stifled laughter as she ushered them out to the bus. Miss Debbie's sisters and their granddaughters were anxiously waiting to help get each girl aboard the bus and strapped into appropriate car seats if needed. When everyone was loaded and ready to go, Miss Debbie introduced the bus driver.

"This wonderful lady has agreed to get us all safely to the church. Please meet a dear friend of mine, Miss Kathy. Let's all give her a hand for agreeing to drive us to the church! Please stand up, Miss Kathy, so all the girls can see you!"

The girls all clapped as Miss Kathy stood up and bowed. She was a small lady with curly red hair and a smile that was aimed in every direction. She had smiling eyes too and wore a big straw hat with flowers all around the brim. She tipped her hat toward the girls and welcomed them aboard! Then she climbed back into her seat, snapped on her seat belt, and they were off!

As they headed to Miss Debbie's church, the girls chatted excitedly! None of them had any idea what to expect, and Sarah could hardly believe this was all in honor of her birthday! Miss Debbie's sister Jill introduced her granddaughter Destani to the girls, and Becky introduced her granddaughter Tahler. They were both friendly and outgoing with the girls, asking questions about the school and talking about their church. Even baby Grace could sense the excitement as she looked with wide eyes at the scenery flashing by. Tahler sat behind her and Sarah and kept reaching over to touch Grace's little fingers and tell her what a pretty baby she was. Lucy and Nora sat in booster seats, one beside Miss Jill and one beside Miss Becky. The women asked them how they were doing and made sure they were comfortable. Lucy cracked everyone up when they heard her tell Miss Jill that she was a big girl now and could go potty all by herself. Miss Jill praised her and told her what a great job she was doing, then whispered to her that she could let her know at any time if she needed to use the bathroom, and she would show her where it was at the church.

Miss Jill's granddaughter Destani sat behind Emma and Sophie, and Sarah heard her asking them what it was like to be a twin. They were shy with her at first, but soon they were chatting away like old friends. Maddi and Gabbi sat together as usual, as did Katie and Kodi. Before they had gone very far, Maddi started singing a song, and soon everyone joined in. "This little light of mine, I'm gonna let it shine, let it shine, let it shine, let it shine!" When they pulled up to the church a few moments later, Miss Kathy stopped the bus in the parking lot, and Miss Debbie turned to all the girls to provide a few directions. She explained that they would go around to the lower level of the church and pointed to a door that they would enter.

"There will be places to hang your jackets and table and chairs for everyone. Please find a seat once you are ready, and dinner will be served by some of our church friends. Let's remember that this is in honor of Miss Sarah's birthday, and let's all make sure she has a very happy evening. I will take baby Grace and look after her tonight so Sarah can enjoy her party. Let's make sure everyone has a buddy, especially the little ones, and go two by two just like Noah's ark." Miss Debbie unbuckled Grace from the car seat and led the way off the bus, saying, "Let's go have some fun, girls!"

Since Sarah didn't have Grace to worry about, and Lucy and Nora each had the other sisters to help them, she hung back watching to make sure each of the girls had a buddy. The twins, Emma and Sophie, were holding hands as they left the bus, and Olivia had paired up with Jill's granddaughter Destani. Gabbi and Maddi followed, with Katie and Kodi close behind them, which left Sarah and Tahler to bring up the rear.

"Are you excited?" Tahler asked her as they left the bus.

"I think so," Sarah answered with a smile. 'It feels weird not being responsible for everyone and trying to make sure each of them has what they need."

Tahler patted her on the shoulder. "Enjoy it," she said. "From what I have heard, you have earned it, and tonight is for you. We will make sure all the girls are fine, but more importantly, have some fun yourself!"

Sarah looked up at Tahler's words and saw the kindness in her eyes. It almost made her start to cry, with everyone being so kind and understanding. She managed a quick thank-you before it was their turn to enter the door and see what this party was all about.

When they got inside, the girls could not believe their eyes! There were balloons and streamers everywhere and a long table down the center of the room with dishes and silverware, and even bibs for the younger girls. The girls couldn't quit staring in amazement as the ladies helped them take off their jackets and hang them on hooks along the wall. At the head of the table was a sign that said "Birthday Girl," which Sarah was ushered toward. As she sat at the head of the table, watching all the other girls take their seats, she was so excited she could hardly stand it. Miss Debbie had already handed baby Grace off to another lady at the church, Miss Jackie, who was sitting in a big rocking chair, snuggling her and making baby noises to her. As Miss Debbie walked around the table making sure everyone was settled and ready for dinner, she carried a little silver crown up to Sarah and placed in on her head. The other girls oohed and ahhed; and suddenly, as it quieted down, Olivia said, "Oh, Sarah, you look lovely." That made everyone start clapping again, and Sarah found herself blushing, never having had this much attention all directed at her.

"Okay, let's get this party started. I would like to give a word of thanks before we eat. Shall we all hold hands and bow our heads?" Each girl reached out to the girl next to them, and their hands formed one big united circle as Miss Debbie bowed her head and began to pray. "Dear Lord, we are gathered here tonight to celebrate Sarah's birthday. Thank you for this opportunity for all of us to join together in honor of her and have fellowship in Your precious name. Thank You for all of Your blessings and for giving these girls someone like Sarah to care for them and teach them about You, God. Bless each one of us gathered here tonight and be with us as we break bread and just have some fun. Thank You for the wonderful friends and helpers who are making this possible and for all that You have provided for this wondrous event. We love You and thank You always, in Your Son's holy name, amen." As a round of amen finished the prayer, Miss Debbie said loudly, "Let the dinner begin!"

Suddenly ladies came out of the kitchen carrying all kinds of dishes and going from girl to girl, asking what they would like. Miss Jeannie, who had organized the food, led them all proudly. There were plates of chicken and mashed potatoes, macaroni and cheese, corn, and green beans. There were homemade rolls and butter and as much milk and juice as the girls wanted. Watching Nora ask Miss Becky if she got to have a whole chicken leg, Sarah smiled. They never had food like this at the school. Sarah herself gobbled up a chicken leg and wing, mashed potatoes with fresh gravy, and even some of both vegetables. And of course, the roll was simply amazing! The little girls made quick work of the food as the church ladies looked on encouragingly. What an awesome dinner!

Soon the girls were all stuffed, and food had been picked up and dishes carried away to the kitchen. When Sarah asked Miss Debbie if they could help with cleanup, she told her, "Absolutely not! This is your day, and there will be no working for any of you." She gathered all the girls over to the other side of the room and sat them in a big area on the floor. "How about some games?" Miss Debbie asked. In response to the chorus of agreement, she nodded to her helpers, and the games began. There was the old faithful pin the tail on the donkey, and there were little buckets that they took turns throwing balls into. Each bucket had a prize, and the helpers made sure even the little ones made at least one bucket. The helpers went around to each of the girls and handed out canvas bags that someone had painted their names on. The girls were in awe at the thoughtful gesture and so excited that they each had their very own bag with their name on it. Sarah knew they would treasure the bags for a long time to come.

After the games were completed, the girls were all asked to take their seats. While they were playing, the ladies had come around and cleaned the table and passed out plates and napkins and drinks. As Sarah took her seat at the head of the table, Miss Debbie came out of the kitchen carrying the biggest birthday cake Sarah had ever seen! It had two layers on top of each other, and there were twelve lighted candles glowing on the top of the cake. As she reached Sarah, Miss Debbie nodded to Maddi, who started singing "Happy Birthday." Soon everyone was singing, and Sarah thought she would die from embarrassment, but she was oh so happy! She made a wish and blew out the candles at the girls' command. Soon the cake was cut and passed around, and ice cream was passed around to all the girls. Even though they were full from the big dinner, the games had worked off some of the food, and none of the girls had any problem at least tasting some of the cake and ice cream. Sarah thought she had never had such a wonderful party in her entire life!

As the plates and leftovers were being cleaned up, the girls began to get up in preparation to get ready to leave. However, Miss Debbie had one more big surprise! She gathered the girls around Sarah as Tahler and Destani carried out a small table from a nearby room and set it down before them. On the table was a row of pretty little bags with ribbons and several presents. Sarah looked on in dismay and turned her questioning eyes to Miss Debbie as they filled with tears.

"N-no!" Sarah stammered. "This is too much!"

"Nonsense," Miss Debbie replied. "You can't have a birthday without presents! And the little goody bags were made by our Sunday school classes for all of you!" The girls started clapping and shouting for Sarah to open her presents. "Before you open your presents, let's have each of the girls come up and give you their card and get their goody bag, okay?" All Sarah could manage was a nod. "Lucy, why don't you come up and give Sarah the birthday card you made her?"

Little Lucy stood up and proudly walked up and picked her card out of the box Miss Debbie was holding and marched right over to Sarah. She held her card up to Sarah and said clearly, "I made this for you, Miss Sarah. It says, 'Happy birthday' and 'I love you' right there in that big red heart. Do you see it?"

"Oh, Lucy, it's beautiful. Thank you so much!" Sarah told her as she gave her a big hug and handed her a goody bag. "Save your goodies for tomorrow, okay?"

Lucy took one look at the goody bag and proudly walked back to her bag with her name on it and placed it inside with the "prizes" she had won.

One by one, the girls came up to Sarah and presented her with their cards. Sarah fussed over each card and hugged the girls and gave them their goody bags. Finally, it was time to open the presents. The girls were almost as excited as Sarah.

There were three presents. The first present was a new journal and a set of colored pens for writing in it. Of course, Sarah loved it. The second gift was a big package that contained a new pair of pajamas, with little black penguins all over them. There was also a fuzzy robe and slippers to match the pajamas. That left one more present, which was also fairly large. When Sarah opened the present, it was a brand-new outfit! The outfit consisted of soft leggings in dark blue with a light-blue tunic-style shirt to go over them. The shirt had tiny navy-blue stars scattered across the material to match the leggings. In addition, there was a warm fleece jacket with a hood! Miss Debbie had seen the jacket that Sarah wore when she went outside to get the mail and knew that Sarah had outgrown it years before but would not ask for another bigger one. There were always too many other things that they all needed.

"Oh, it's so beautiful!" Sarah said as she held the jacket up to her cheek. "And so soft!" She ran over and hugged Miss Debbie, hiding her tears from the others.

"Okay, girls, we are already running a bit late, so let's use the bathroom if necessary and round everything up so we can get you home." She patted Sarah on the shoulder as everyone else came up to admire her presents. And of course, there was a goody bag for Sarah as well.

"Oooh, I love your outfit and the jacket!" Tahler said as she came up to see the presents. They all admired her pajamas and robe and slippers as she packed them back in the boxes to go on the bus. She kept out the jacket to wear home. Now she could give her old jacket to Katie as hers was also way too small. She walked over where hers was hanging and whispered to Katie. Katie was thrilled to have the larger jacket and put it on immediately, stuffing the other one in her bag.

After many hugs and good-byes, the girls were all finally loaded on the bus with all their helpers. Baby Grace had fallen asleep, and little Lucy and Nora were both rubbing their eyes as the bus started the journey toward home. Sarah sat next to the sleeping baby, thinking about the wonderful evening that had just transpired. She felt very emotional, and she knew without question that this was a gift from God. She prayed silently, thanking Him for His many blessing and sending out love to her parents, praying that somehow they knew and shared in her happiness. She felt better than she could ever remember feeling.

8

MADDI HUMMED SOFTLY ON the way home, but most of
the girls were quiet in the darkened bus. They were all worn
out from all the food and treats and excitement. Sarah knew
they would all sleep soundly that night.

As the bus pulled up to the Heavenly Home for Girls,
Miss Kathy whispered something to Miss Debbie, who
commented on the fact that there was no light on in the
building. Mrs. Harper had promised to wait up for them
and leave the outside light on. Once the bus came to a
complete stop, Miss Debbie asked that all the girls stay
seated while she checked with Mrs. Harper. She left the
bus and walked up the steps to the building. When no one
answered her knock on the door, she came back and asked
Miss Jill to come with her to check things out. She had a
key to the building so she wouldn't have to bother Mrs.
Harper when she came to provide lessons, so getting inside
was not a problem. The girls were all starting to chatter and
question what was going on, so Sarah reassured them that

all was fine and asked Maddi to start a song. Soon most of the girls were singing along. Sarah looked back at Tahler, wondering what she thought of it all; but Tahler shrugged her shoulders and shook her head, indicating that she had no idea.

Suddenly the lights came on in the building, and Miss Debbie and Miss Jill could be seen inside as they made their way through the rooms, turning on lights as they went. Sarah noticed when the upstairs lights came on and breathed a little easier when Miss Debbie and Miss Jill came back outside and made their way to the bus. Miss Debbie informed them all that Mrs. Harper had to leave unexpectedly, and she would be staying with them until Mrs. Harper returned. She asked all the girls to pick up their belongings and make their way carefully out of the bus. Once the girls were all inside, Sarah ushered them carefully up the stairs, where they each placed their prizes in their drawers or boxes. Miss Debbie had carried Grace upstairs and gently laid her in her crib as she was fast asleep. Sarah scurried around, helping Lucy and Nora into their pajamas. They were both worn out from all the excitement and were soon in their beds, fast asleep. Once the rest of the girls were changed into pajamas, Miss Debbie suggested they come downstairs while she talked with her sisters and made arrangements to get the bus back to the church. The girls looked at one another with surprised expressions but quietly followed Miss Debbie down the stairs.

Miss Debbie led the girls to the parlor where they got in their usual circle on the big rug in front of the couch. Miss Becky and Tahler were there as well, but Miss Jill and Destani had decided to go with Miss Kathy to take the bus back to the church and go on home. Sarah could sense her confusion as Miss Debbie told the girls they would all work together until Mrs. Harper returned to the school. She noticed the looks from Miss Becky and Tahler and knew there was more to the story. However, she also knew the girls would be upset if they thought something was wrong, so she listened and nodded with the rest of them.

Miss Debbie informed them she would stay the night and be there until there was more information. She suggested they all come downstairs tomorrow for breakfast and asked what they would like. The girls looked at Sarah as they had never been asked that question before. Sarah quickly told Miss Debbie that they could just eat cereal upstairs as they usually did, but Miss Debbie was hearing none of it. She insisted the girls come downstairs and asked the girls if they liked pancakes and sausage. Seven little hands went up in the air, and finally Sarah added hers as well. Miss Debbie beamed and told the girls that Miss Becky and Tahler had agreed to spend the night as well and have breakfast with them. The girls all stood up to give them hugs and promised to go right to sleep! They could hardly wait for the promised breakfast. As the tired girls trudged back up the stairs, Sarah turned to Miss Debbie with a hug and thanks of her own. The party was amazing, and now they had breakfast to look forward to. It was definitely her best birthday *ever*!

In the morning, baby Grace woke them all up with her gurgling. She was chewing on her fingers and looking up at the animals above her. The girls woke up one by one and started chattering among themselves, laughing at baby Grace. Sarah yawned and stretched as she climbed out of bed. She encouraged all the girls to make their beds and get dressed and be ready to go down for breakfast. The yummy smells were already drifting up the stairs, so the girls needed little encouragement to get going. Soon they all stood in a line, waiting impatiently for Miss Sarah to check their beds and the bathroom. Everything was neat and tidy, so Sarah picked up baby Grace, along with the bottle she had prepared earlier, and they all headed downstairs.

Miss Becky's granddaughter Tahler was waiting for them at the bottom of the stairs and directed them toward the dining room. The table seated twelve, and Sarah had always wondered why they weren't allowed to eat there. Mrs. Harper had always preferred they eat upstairs. The girls all took their places at the table, with Miss Tahler putting cushions from the couch under the two little ones to make them high enough. Miss Becky came over and took baby Grace from Sarah and offered to give her the bottle Sarah had prepared. Sarah sat down with the girls, a bit in awe of the whole experience.

Within a few minutes, Miss Debbie came out of the kitchen with a huge platter of pancakes and went around the table putting them on the girls' plates. Butter and syrup were passed around by Tahler, who helped the little ones put it on their pancakes. Once everyone had pancakes, Miss Debbie returned to the kitchen and came back with a platter of sausages, which were also passed around to all. Once they all had their food, Miss Debbie encouraged them to eat!

"But wait!" Olivia exclaimed. "We have to pray!" All the girls put their hands together and bowed their heads to pray. Olivia carefully started the prayer, "God is great. God is good. Let us thank Him for our food. Amen."

With much excitement, the girls all picked up their silverware and began to gobble up their amazing breakfast! Tahler passed around juice and milk to those who wanted it, and soon almost all the girls had clean plates. Miss Debbie walked around wiping sticky hands and faces and making sure everyone had enough to eat. She praised the girls for their manners and suggested that they all help carry dishes out to the kitchen so they could be rinsed and stacked in the dishwasher. The girls looked at Sarah, who smiled and stood up, gathering her plate, cup, and silverware and standing up to carry it to the kitchen. Soon the other girls followed her example, carrying their dishes out to the kitchen and hurrying back to help the littlest girls. Miss Debbie marveled at the fact that they didn't have to be told to help them but worked together as a sort of family, making sure everyone was taken care of.

Once all the dishes had been carried to the kitchen, Miss Debbie suggested they all go into the parlor and find something to watch on the television. Dutifully, the girls filed into the parlor and found a place to sit while Sarah fumbled with the channel, looking for something entertaining. She found a cartoon channel, and soon the girls were chatting and giggling about the cartoons. Miss Becky stood up from the chair where she was sitting with baby Grace and handed her to Sarah so she could go in and help Tahler and Miss Debbie in the kitchen. Sarah looked around at the girls and smiled. She couldn't remember a time when they had all enjoyed the parlor so much! After a few minutes, the phone in the office rang, and Miss Debbie came out of the kitchen, through the dining room and parlor, and hurried into the office to answer it. Sarah waited nervously, wondering if it was Mrs. Harper. She would not be happy to see them all in the parlor watching cartoons.

When Miss Debbie came out of the office, she smiled at the girls and suggested they take Grace upstairs for a nap as she had fallen asleep on Sarah's lap. Tahler and Miss Becky had joined the girls and were gathering them together to play some games. Sarah stood up stiffly from her position on the floor, carefully lifting the sleeping baby, and headed upstairs with Miss Debbie. Once she placed Grace in the crib, Miss Debbie sat down on Sarah's bed and motioned her to join her. She explained that the call had been the police reporting on the missing-person case that Miss Debbie had called in that morning. It seemed that Mrs. Harper was simply gone. The police had gone to her neighbors asking about her, and someone told them she packed up her car and headed out shortly after the girls had left for the party. It appeared she had driven away with no intention to return that night. The girls were left like unwanted clothing, with no one to care for them. Tears rolled down Sarah's cheeks as she tried to understand what this meant to all the girls. Would they have to leave the school? Who would take them? Would they be separated?

Miss Debbie tried to comfort Sarah, patting her gently and reminding her that there still might be more to the story. The police were still investigating and would fill them in when they had more. Finally, she took her hand. "Sarah, remember Miss Jackie and Miss Jeannie from our church last night?" Sarah nodded her head, acknowledging that she remembered, and tried to sniff her tears away. "I just spoke with them on the phone, and they are willing to come and stay with all of you until we sort this out. I will still come and teach as I always have, and we will try to keep things as close to your normal routine as possible. How does that sound?" Miss Debbie waited patiently while Sarah tried to gain her composure.

"Can we really do that?" Sarah asked with a doubtful tone.

"I believe we can," Miss Debbie answered. "I have talked with both CPS and the police department. They are willing to put all of you in their care until they sort through the papers in the office. They are both approved foster parents and are willing to take you all in as long as they can do it here. This building is paid for, and all utility and service bills have been set up to be paid automatically from an account that Mrs. Harper set up years ago. There is more than enough money to cover expenses as it seems Mrs. Harper left quite a bit of money behind." Miss Debbie paused, giving Sarah time to take this all in.

Sarah looked over at the sleeping baby who had become dear to her over the past month, and nodded her head. "As long as we can all stay together," she said.

Miss Debbie suggested that she and Sarah keep this between the two of them and just tell the other girls that the church ladies were going to stay with them until Mrs. Harper returned. She assured Sarah that she would be there any time Sarah needed her and was just a phone call away. She also talked to Sarah about the CPS questions in her note and told Sarah she was checking into it but was pretty sure it would continue until Sarah turned eighteen. As one of the girls called for Sarah from downstairs, Miss Debbie encouraged her to join the others and wait until bedtime to share the news. She offered to stay upstairs with baby Grace, informing Sarah that she still had several phone calls to make. She gave Sarah a hug and sent her on her way.

As the girls got ready for bed that night, Sarah shared the news that Miss Jeannie and Miss Jackie were going to come over to take care of them until Mrs. Harper was located. The girls were still a bit confused with everything that had been happening since they returned from the party, but Miss Jeannie and Miss Jackie has been so nice at the church party that none of them had any reservations about the ladies coming to take care of them.

"Is Mrs. Harper gone forever?" asked Olivia quietly.

"We don't know yet," Sarah replied. "We'll just have to wait and see." Sarah saw a couple of the older girls looking at each other with raised eyebrows, but she ignored it. "It's been a very long but fun couple of days, so let's just say our prayers and get some sleep." Sarah made her usual round to listen to the girls' prayers and peeked over at baby Grace, who was sleeping soundly. Miss Debbie had given her a bath and fed her before the girls came upstairs, so she was all set for the night.

During prayers, Sarah was surprised to hear many of the girls pray for Mrs. Harper to be okay. In spite of her meanness to them at times, she was still their provider, and the girls did not want harm to come to her. Sarah crawled into her bed at last, worried about all that was happening. Still, as she drifted off to sleep, it was the wonderful birthday party that filled her dreams.

9

MORNING CAME WITH THE unusual smell of cooking. The girls scurried around getting dressed, brushing teeth, and making beds. They couldn't help but anticipate another wonderful breakfast at the big table in the dining room. Sarah changed Grace and passed her to Katie with a fresh bottle of milk. She hurried to get herself ready and make her own bed, and had just finished when the girls heard the tinkling of a bell and a sweet voice saying, "Breakfast is ready! Come on down, girls!" Sarah had never seen the girls so excited for breakfast before and so eager to go downstairs. Today there were fresh warm cinnamon rolls and little sausages and a big bowl of fresh red strawberries!

February and March flew by, and the atmosphere finally matched the name of the school. The Heavenly Home for Girls had become just that: a heavenly place to be. Meals were all shared in the dining room now, and the girls were even learning to cook and bake. Miss Jeannie and Miss Jackie loved helping them create new meals and bake cookies and cupcakes. Even the little girls took part in stirring and adding ingredients and helping to decorate the baked goods. The girls now spent their days in the main "parlor" of the house, playing games, watching movies, and helping with chores. Miss Jackie and Miss Jeannie told amazing stories, and Sarah had not heard so much laughter in all of the time she had been at the school. The girls still went upstairs for lessons three days a week, but even that was more relaxed. The girls were starting to thrive!

Sarah blossomed under Miss Debbie's guidance, finally getting to spend more time on her own studies, and even managed to squeeze in a couple of hours here and there to read a book in a quiet corner. Miss Debbie had loaned her *Anne of Green Gables*, which she loved! She was still the main caregiver for baby Grace, but all the other girls helped too. Miss Jackie loved rocking Grace and singing to her while the girls were busy with lessons. And Grace was blossoming herself! She was starting to be more alert and could roll over and sit up by herself. She could hold small toys and was starting to eat baby food! The girls loved to put her in her high chair and feed her! Mrs. Rogers from CPS continued to visit them, always bringing goodies for the girls and diapers, formula, and clothes for baby Grace. She was thrilled with the change in the atmosphere of the school and brought other things for the girls as well. Often she surprised them with extra food, a new game or puzzle, and even clothes for the girls, who were outgrowing what they had. When someone got a new outfit or jacket or shoes, everyone was happy because they passed what they had outgrown to someone else. With all the different shapes and sizes of girls, they could usually make use of everything.

Mr. Frank stopped by too just to make sure they were all okay. He fixed a cracked window, repaired a leaky faucet, and took care of anything he could to make the house a better place for the girls. He almost always had a little something for the girls: dolls for the little ones, coloring books and crayons, and pens and journals for the older girls. Once he even stayed to have dinner with them. Even baby Grace got excited when Mr. Frank came by and would fuss a bit until he picked her up and showed her some attention. He would tickle her or toss her up in the air until she was laughing out loud!

April brought some warmer weather, and the girls started clamoring to go outside. One day, a group of ladies came by from Miss Debbie's church and had tea with the girls. Miss Jackie and Miss Jeannie got out all the cups and saucers and made pretend tea (apple juice) for all the girls, serving cupcakes that the girls had decorated the night before. Sarah watched nervously as even the little girls were given teacups. She still worried about what Mrs. Harper would say if she were there and what would happen to the school if she returned. She was afraid it would not be good. The girls were very careful with the teacups, and they got through tea without as much as a cracked cup or plate.

Later in the week, the ladies came back to the school with new spring dresses and jackets for each of the girls, even Grace! They had noted the girls' sizes when they came for tea and their women's group had collected and donated enough money to cover the cost. For once, every girl had something brand-new! And the ladies invited all the girls to wear their new dresses and come to church for Easter Sunday!

The girls rose early Easter morning and gathered around Sarah as she read the Easter story from her faithful Bible. Sarah explained that the most important thing about Easter is that Jesus willingly died to take away all of our sins or wrongdoings and bring us closer to God, and that He came back to life three days later and is still alive today in heaven. The girls listened intently as they always did when Sarah got out her Bible. They knew how much she cherished the one thing she had from her parents, so they had learned to treasure the times she shared it with them. Once they had finished the story and all the questions that followed it, they made their beds and were hovering around baby Grace, waiting for the tinkling of the bell that Miss Jackie and Miss Jeannie used to let them know that breakfast was ready. Grace was talking in her sweet gurgling baby talk as the girls took turns telling her good morning and giving her love. They stayed in their pajamas since it was still early, planning to wait and get dressed after breakfast. As soon as they heard the bell, they lined up and headed down the stairs, with Sarah and baby Grace leading them all.

As the girls made their way into the parlor on their way to the dining room, a wondrous sight met their eyes! Lined up across the sofa were eleven little Easter baskets full of goodies! Most of the girls had never even seen an Easter basket, let alone ever had one. Miss Jackie and Miss Jeannie stood at the door of the dining room, watching the girls' expressions with big smiles on their faces. They clapped their hands at the girls' excitement and encouraged them to come in for breakfast, which was almost as special as the baskets. There were scrambled eggs and crisp bacon, along with fresh hot cross buns! As they all got into their places, Miss Debbie arrived to join them for breakfast. Miss Debbie shared the story of hot cross buns, and explained that a monk baked the buns and marked them with a cross in honor of Good Friday. Over time they gained popularity, and eventually became a symbol of Easter weekend. After answering the girls' questions and explaining what Good Friday referred to and what a monk was, all the girls had a taste. Everyone agreed that hot cross buns tasted wonderful! The girls had gotten comfortable eating in the dining room over the past couple of months, and the happy chatter and laughter had become routine.

Once the girls had finished breakfast, they carried all their dishes into the kitchen to be loaded into the dishwasher. They kept peeking through the dining room into the parlor at the baskets, anxious to see what was inside. Miss Jeannie and Miss Jackie were as excited as they were, and as soon as the last item was carried into the kitchen, they told the girls to go into the parlor and form a circle on the floor. The girls almost ran into the parlor, and within seconds, they were in a big circle on the floor. Miss Debbie had picked up baby Grace to snuggle with her, so Sarah joined the girls. Miss Jackie and Miss Jeannie made a big deal out of picking up each of the baskets and trying to figure out whom it belonged to. They watched as the girls' faces lit up when they realized a basket was theirs! They had spent a good deal of time figuring out special little treats for each of the girls, including a sparkly bracelet for Gabbi and a small musical book for Maddi. Each of the girls also received some sort of reminder about God, such as Lucy's little stuffed lamb that played "Jesus loves me" and Sarah's necklace with a pretty gold cross. Soon it was time to get ready for church, so the girls piled their goodies back into their baskets and headed upstairs to get ready.

The church bus arrived right on time, and all the girls were ready and excited to go to church. They came down the stairs like a rainbow—Sarah and baby Grace in lavender, Lucy in pink, Nora in peach, Olivia in pale blue, Emma and Sophie in aqua (of course, they had matching dresses!), Maddi in yellow, Gabbi in mint green, Katie in rose, and Kodi in purple. Miss Jill and Destani and Miss Becky and Tahler had arrived while they were getting ready and were happy to see all the girls again and join them for church. They all climbed in the bus and found their places as they had before. Miss Kathy popped open the bus doors and was smiling brightly as the girls filed onto the bus. Once everyone was in their places, Miss Kathy closed the door, and away they all went!

When they arrived at the church, they made quite a sensation! The bus stopped right at the front of the church, and the girls walked into the church two by two as they had the night of Sarah's party. Miss Debbie led the way and found two empty pews that would seat all of them. As the girls were seated, the adults made sure that the little ones had someone to sit with them during the service. The older girls had paired up as they had before, and once again, Sarah found herself seated next to Tahler. There was excited chatter throughout the church, and the girls began to chat as well. Finally, the pastor walked up to the front of the church and said in a loud voice, "Christ is risen!" The entire congregation stood up and responded by saying. "Christ is risen indeed!" Soon everyone was taking their seats, and the church quieted until all you could hear was an occasional whisper.

The pastor began telling the story of Easter and Jesus dying for our sins. At one point in the sermon, Sarah heard Sophie whisper, "It's just like Sarah said!" She looked over and smiled at her, putting her finger to her lips to remind her to be quiet. The girls loved the songs and tried to sing along when they could. All too soon, the service was over, and it was time to go. Sarah felt a little sad as they all filed out, until she heard Maddi say, "This is the *best* Easter ever!" Suddenly it all felt exactly right! Christ had risen indeed, and God's grace was all around them!

The girls were introduced to multiple people in the congregation, shaking hands and smiling and generally feeling part of the atmosphere of new life and new beginnings. Grace had fallen asleep on Miss Becky's shoulder, and soon it was time to get back on the bus to return home. As they filed out of the church, Miss Kathy pulled up right on cue and popped open the doors of the bus, ready for them with a big smile on her face! The girls scrambled up the steps of the bus and took their seats for the return trip. When they got back to the school, the first thing the girls recognized was Mr. Frank's truck. Sure enough, he was waiting for them and jumped out to greet them as they got off the bus. It seemed that Mr. Frank had been up to his own Easter mischief while they were at church. He had brought over one hundred Easter eggs and hidden them outside all around the school grounds. He encouraged the girls to change out of their good dresses as soon as possible and come outside for a big Easter egg hunt!

Miss Jeannie and Miss Jackie welcomed them back and hurried them upstairs to change. Miss Becky laid Grace on the sofa with a big pillow in front of her, so Sarah went upstairs with the other girls to change clothes. Tahler and Destani came upstairs as well to help Lucy and Nora change. The girls chattered and giggled in excitement as they got out of their new dresses. Sarah hung each of their dresses on hangers in preparation for hanging them in the closet downstairs. They were all so pretty! Within minutes, the girls were changed and ready to go down for the Easter egg hunt.

Mr. Frank explained that each of the girls got to find ten of the brightly colored plastic eggs. He handed each of the girls a bag, reminding the older girls to let the little ones find the eggs that were in plain sight. They all laughed at the little ones, who squealed with joy each time they picked up an egg! Once each of the girls had ten eggs in their bag, they all went inside to open the eggs. The eggs were filled with little toys and candies, and all the girls had fun comparing their treasures. They thanked Mr. Frank again and again for the wonderful surprise. Afterward, the little ones went upstairs for a nap while the older girls put all the eggs back together for Mr. Frank. With final hugs and a big thank-you, they sent him on his way with fresh hot cross buns. It certainly was the best Easter ever!

10

MAY AND JUNE WERE warm and sunny, and so was the Heavenly Home for Girls! Grace was starting to pull herself up to things in preparation for trying her first tentative steps. Sarah smiled and thought she would be walking in no time, with all the help and encouragement from the girls. And school had become more like "crafts" for the summer. The girls could not bear life without Miss Debbie, so she came three times a week anyway and just kept the lessons fun and light. And the house was a different place now, with color and light and laughter—until July 15, when they got the call.

The girls were all around the table in the dining room, frosting and decorating their latest batch of cookies, when the phone rang. It was a Friday, so Miss Debbie was there and had declared "learning to decorate cookies" their lesson for the day. She went in the office to answer the call, and when she came out afterward, the look on her face said it all: something was very wrong!

Miss Debbie quickly gained her composure and went back to decorating cookies, but the older girls knew there was a problem. Once they had finished with the cookies, Miss Jeannie and Miss Jackie suggested taking the little ones upstairs to wash up and have a story and nap. They took Gracie, Lucy, and Nora upstairs, with Olivia stating solemnly that she was almost seven and should stay with the older girls. Once they were gone, Miss Debbie got serious.

That was the police on the phone, she informed them. They had found Mrs. Harper. She had been in the hospital and a rehabilitation center in a nearby town. She had been very ill, but she was getting stronger. And she wanted to come home. The girls all looked at Miss Debbie in horror! "Noooo!" exclaimed Emma and Sophie in perfect unison. Olivia started to cry quietly, and Maddi rushed over to comfort her, trying not to cry herself. Miss Debbie looked at Sarah and then around at all the girls. She really didn't know what to say.

After a brief silence, Sarah spoke quietly, "We don't really have a say in this, girls, because, after all, this is Mrs. Harper's school and home. Without her, we would not all be together in the first place. Maybe if we show her how well we have been doing, she will let us keep doing things the way we are doing them. Maybe she even needs our help." Sarah was hesitant because she knew it was really out of their hands. If Mrs. Harper came back and wanted the girls to go back to staying upstairs, no one could stop it.

"Why did Mrs. Harper leave us that night?" Sarah asked Miss Debbie, referring to the night of her birthday party.

Miss Debbie explained that Mrs. Harper had been taking some things to her friend Rachel who lived nearby when she got in a horrible accident. She was pulled from her car unconscious and was taken to a hospital where she was in critical condition for months, with a broken leg and a concussion.

"Her car caught on fire in the accident, right after she was removed from it, and everything was burned, including her identification," Miss Debbie went on to explain. "It took her friend a long time to find her. She is still having trouble with her memory of the past, but her friend Rachel, who finally found her, is trying to help her with details. Thankfully, everything is in place to pay for the expenses of the school automatically through an online account with her bank, so there has been no real impact to the school."

Except that it is so much better without her, thought Sarah sadly.

After the initial shock, the girls were beginning to settle down to the fact that Mrs. Harper might return. While they had loved all the changes in her absence, it had not seemed like reality, and most of them knew it might not last. Once Miss Debbie saw that the girls were starting to accept the news, she encouraged them about the future. After all, they had been doing okay until the party, and she reminded them that her church was going to stay involved unless Mrs. Harper strictly forbade it, which Miss Debbie did not think she would do. She promised to put in a good word for them as she and Mrs. Harper had been friends long ago. She told the girls that she was planning to visit Mrs. Harper over the weekend and would like Sarah to go with her. Also, believe it or not, Mrs. Harper had been mentioning the baby at the rehabilitation center where she was staying, and the staff there thought it would be nice if they could bring her along to see Mrs. Harper. It seemed she was starting to remember bits and pieces of her past, and they were hoping the visit would help bring it back. Sarah agreed to go, and she promised to let the other girls know what she thought when she returned.

The girls decided to put in a movie that Miss Jackie had brought them, and Sarah and Miss Debbie were both happy to see the girls distracted from the news about Mrs. Harper. Miss Debbie went into the kitchen to make them all popcorn, and soon they were all chatting and enjoying the movie. The popcorn was a special treat for the girls, and it was fun to see the older girls adjusting their usual pairings to include Olivia. Katie and Kodi had matched up with the twins for a change, and Maddi and Gabbi had Olivia sandwiched in between them, sharing their bowl of popcorn. These girls were such sweeties, and Miss Debbie's heart hurt for them. More changes in the near future were inevitable! She was already praying that everything would work out for the best.

The next day, Sarah awoke early and got dressed for her outing to visit Mrs. Harper. The girls had become more relaxed with their morning routine over the past months, and it was nice to see them take a little more time waking up and getting around. There were no more morning inspections, no constant criticism, and the school had truly become a happy place to live. Sarah heard Grace gurgling in her crib and went over and picked up the little girl. Her light-brown curls were getting longer, and her blue eyes were bright this morning. Sarah took her into the bathroom and put some warm water and baby soap in the tub where she had recently started bathing her as the plastic bathtub was getting too small, and Grace made a mess splashing in the water. Once Grace was scrubbed and dried, Sarah dressed her and put a few things together for her trip. She was feeding Grace a fresh bottle when the other girls started waking up. Sarah sat and watched her little brood as, one by one, they woke up to face a new day.

Miss Debbie picked up Sarah and Grace after breakfast, and they headed to the rehabilitation center where Mrs. Harper was staying. Grace gurgled away in her car seat as they chatted. Miss Debbie told Sarah about a program in the fall she was teaching that she would like her to attend in the evenings. It was a creative writing class for high school–aged girls, but with Sarah's advanced abilities in reading and writing, Miss Debbie felt Sarah would do fine. Besides, she was sure Sarah would probably have advanced to high school classes by now anyway in normal circumstances. Sarah was excited and apprehensive at the same time. Even though Miss Debbie would pick her up and take her to the classes, she was unsure of the impact Mrs. Harper would have on everything. As they pulled up to the rehab center, Sarah started to feel a little sick at the thought of seeing Mrs. Harper.

Miss Debbie helped Sarah get Grace out of her car seat, and they headed into the center. Miss Debbie inquired about the visit, and a smiling volunteer led them down the hall to Mrs. Harper's room. When they stepped inside the door to her room, Sarah was sure they had made a mistake. They had to be in the wrong room. The woman sitting up in the bed, with dark hair down around her shoulders, did not look like the Mrs. Harper she remembered. With a cast on her leg and several scratches and bruises on her face, she looked a little like a younger version of the woman. Mrs. Harper looked questioningly at the girls as they slowly entered her room. Finally, she said quietly, "Hi, Debbie and Sarah. Please come in."

Miss Debbie handed Grace to Sarah and walked over to the bed. "Hello, Maree."

Sarah stared at both of them. Maree? Since when was Mrs. Harper named Maree? Sarah could not believe her eyes and ears. As someone new arrived at her door, Sarah turned to see a black-haired woman enter the room. She walked up to Miss Debbie and shook her hand. "Hello," she said. "My name is Rachel. I am a friend of Maree's.

She told me that you are a teacher and have been working with the girls at the school. And you must be Sarah," she said, turning toward Sarah and reaching out to shake her hand. "And this little cutie has to be the baby I have heard all about!"

"Grace. Her name is Grace," Sarah said. Her mind was reeling as she saw Mrs. Harper looking at them with a smile. What was going on? Where was the ornery old woman that the girls were accustomed to? How did this woman know all about a baby whom she had only grudgingly accepted into her home? Something was very weird here.

Mrs. Harper held her arms out for the baby. Hesitantly, Sarah walked over to her; and to her surprise, Grace went to her without a fuss. Mrs. Harper hugged the little girl to her like she had loved her all along. "Thank you so much for bringing her to see me," Mrs. Harper said in a very nice voice. "Seeing you both makes me happy to be alive!"

Rachel walked over to the bed and gently touched Grace's hair, marveling at her pretty brown curls and blue eyes. Sarah looked at Miss Debbie, who looked surprised as well. She shrugged her shoulders just a bit to indicate she had no idea what was going on. Finally, Mrs. Harper motioned to Sarah to come closer. As soon as Sarah got near the bed, baby Grace reached for her with a smile. Sarah took the baby and hesitated by the bed.

Mrs. Harper was beginning to look a bit worn out, but she reached out a hand and patted Sarah's arm with a puzzled expression. "You are such a good helper, aren't you?" she questioned. "Are Sophie and Emma doing okay?"

Sarah did not know what to say. The tone suggested praise, and the look of the woman lying in the bed just did not make sense. And she could not remember a single time when Mrs. Harper had asked about the twins in the past. She backed away from the bed with Grace and stood next to Miss Debbie. Miss Debbie put her arm around the girls. "I think Maree has had enough visiting time for today," she said. "Maybe we can come back another time." Rachel agreed with Miss Debbie as Mrs. Harper smiled and almost immediately drifted off to sleep. They all said their good-byes and headed out the door.

Back in the car, Sarah was quiet as they headed back to the school. Grace had already fallen asleep in her car seat before they got out of the center's parking lot. Miss Debbie glanced at Sarah and asked her if she was okay. Sarah nodded her head but suddenly blurted out, "What happened to Mrs. Harper? Why is she being so nice? Why did you call her Maree?"

Miss Debbie shook her head sadly, knowing this was hard for Sarah and understanding how confusing it must be for the girl. She told Sarah that the reason Mrs. Harper had contacted her about teaching at the school was because they had been friends in college. Back then, Mrs. Harper was more carefree, and life had not been as difficult as it was now. She was very social, loved children, and was always talking about running a home for girls. Since Miss Debbie was taking classes to become a teacher, they talked often about working together in the future. She went on to tell Sarah that Mrs. Harper had a serious boyfriend and was hoping to get married after college, start her own family, and put aside money to eventually start a school for girls. After college, things went pretty well for Mrs. Harper, and soon she was married and had her first baby on the way. Miss Debbie was in the wedding, and it was a wonderful celebration. She was happy for the newlyweds and knew that Mrs. Harper's dreams were all coming true. Several years later, after Mrs. Harper's daughter, little Lynsey, arrived, she lost touch with Mrs. Harper. Miss Debbie was busy teaching and trying to keep up with her own family, and they didn't see each other for almost thirty years, except for an occasional phone call or card.

When they finally reconnected, Mrs. Harper was a very different person. Miss Debbie discovered that Mrs. Harper could never have more children after Lynsey due to complications during childbirth. As a result, she had lavished all her love on her husband and daughter. They planned a big celebration for their daughter's graduation from college, but on the way home from graduation, there was a terrible accident. Mrs. Harper had driven separately so she could leave a bit early to prepare for their guests. Her husband and daughter were riding together in another vehicle when a car ran a stoplight and hit them head on.

Both were killed instantly. Mrs. Harper was devastated and mourned their deaths for many years.

When she finally met Sophie and Emma's father, she thought things might turn around for her. She married him and was happy to help him care for the little girls, but they only had a short time together before he became ill and was diagnosed with a rare type of cancer. Once again, she found herself alone; this time, with two little girls who reminded her of all she had lost. It was simply more than she could handle, and she became bitter and disillusioned with life. She had all the money she could ever use but nobody to spend it on. A short time later, she decided to go ahead and open her school for girls, but she could not get rid of the bitterness and anger from losing everyone important to her; and unfortunately, she pushed the twins away as a result. Then CPS called her about you, and she found a way to detach herself from them as well. She let you take care of them and pulled away from her love for them.

Sarah had been listening intently to the story, but they were almost back to the school, so Miss Debbie suggested that they talk more at another time. "Let's go have some fun with the girls now, shall we?" She looked closely at Sarah and asked her if she was going to be okay.

Sarah slowly nodded yes and was quiet as they pulled in at the school. Miss Debbie picked up the sleeping baby and carried her inside and up to her crib as Sarah went to see what the other girls were doing. She saw that the girls were all outside with Miss Jackie and Miss Jeannie. Miss Debbie came downstairs and said she had to get going, so Sarah decided to go upstairs herself and do a little reading. She got out her Bible, which she hadn't been using as much, and decided to look for a story to share with the girls in preparation for telling them about Mrs. Harper. She needed to find some encouragement for herself as well.

That night, when all the girls were ready for bed, she asked them if they would like her to read a story from her Bible like she used to before all the changes came. A big chorus of yeses was heard around the room, so Sarah got out her Bible and sat on her bed to start the story. "Titus 2:11–12 says, 'For the grace of God has appeared, bringing salvation for all people, training us to renounce ungodliness and worldly passions, and to live self-controlled, upright, and godly lives in the present age.'" Sarah looked around the room at all the trusting faces watching her and decided to share her own version of the story tonight, changing it a bit to fit the situation with Mrs. Harper. She started out with a question, "Do any of you know what the grace of God means?"

Maddi's hand shot up in the air at the same time she started talking. "Grace is what God gave Noah so he wouldn't drown in the flood," she said confidently.

"You are right, Maddi," Sarah replied. "But why does God give us grace?" she asked.

Kodi spoke next. "God gives us grace because we believe in Him and know that His Son, Jesus, died for our sins," she said solemnly. "Even though we still do the wrong things sometimes, if we admit we are wrong, God will forgive us, and we will still go to heaven to be with Him when we die because we believe His Son already died for our sins. God's grace allows us to still have eternal life if we just believe in Him."

"That is exactly right, Kodi," exclaimed Sarah. "You explained it very well." Kodi beamed. Sarah continued with the story, "We don't always know why people do what they do, but it really isn't for us to decide who is good and who is bad. We only need to worry about our own beliefs and actions, and God will take care of the rest, right?" She looked around the room as most of the girls nodded. "Sometimes we judge others by their actions toward us, even though we don't know their beliefs or anything about what has happened to them. I want to tell you all about seeing Mrs. Harper today."

Suddenly Sarah had every one of the girls' attention. Even little Lucy was wide-eyed and listening. She explained to the girls that Mrs. Harper had a broken leg and a very bad head injury and was having trouble remembering things that had happened in the past. "She looks and acts quite differently," she stated.

"Is she still mean?" Olivia said seriously.

"I really don't know for sure. She was nice to me and Grace," Sarah replied. "She asked about the twins. She would like you to come and see her next time." Now Sarah had scared looks from both Sophie and Emma. "Don't worry," Sarah said as she saw their expressions. "You only go if you want to. I just ask that you all remember that we are together here because Mrs. Harper let each of us come to her school. Even if she seemed grouchy about it, we wouldn't be here without her permission. Now let's say our prayers and get some sleep, okay?"

Sarah went from bed to bed and listened to the girls' prayers. When she got to little Lucy, the little girl looked at her solemnly and said, "I hope Mrs. Harper's broken leg gets better. Do you think she cried when she broke it?" Sarah gave Lucy a hug as she tucked her in and told her that everybody cries sometimes and she was sure that Mrs. Harper cried a little. So Lucy prayed that Mrs. Harper's leg would get better real soon, even if she was a little bit mean!

11

LATER THE NEXT WEEK, Miss Debbie mentioned another visit to see Mrs. Harper, wondering if the twins would like to go this time. Emma looked worried but said bravely, "I will go if Sarah can come too."

"Of course, Sarah will come," Miss Debbie replied.

Sophie was instantly at Emma's side, saying she would go too, so they made plans to go see her the very next day. Miss Jackie and Miss Jeannie agreed to take care of Grace, but they decided to go during the little girl's nap time to make it a little easier. The older girls were good about helping out with the little ones, so they assured them all that it would be fine.

The next day, right after lunch, Miss Debbie came by to pick up the girls. Sophie and Emma were a little bit nervous but also excited to be going with Sarah on the visit. Once Miss Debbie had greeted the other girls and spoken with Miss Jackie and Miss Jeannie, they were on their way. Miss Debbie chatted about the weather on the way to the center, but the girls were pretty quiet on the drive. When they arrived at the center, Miss Debbie parked and led the twins to the front door. Sarah followed, trying to smile her encouragement.

When they got to Mrs. Harper's room, Rachel was already there, waiting to greet them. "My name is Rachel," she said. "You must be Sophie and Emma, but which one is which?"

Rachel tried to put the little girls at ease, but Emma (who almost always took the lead) still stammered slightly as she said, "I-I'm Emma, and this is Sophie. Sophie has the curly hair." As they stepped forward, they noticed the lady on the bed who was smiling at them. Her hair was brushed backed and tied with a hair band, but she still looked much different than the girls remembered.

"Hello, girls," Mrs. Harper spoke from the bed. "How are you doing?"

"Fine," the girls said in unison. They both looked over at Sarah, who stepped closer to them. Mrs. Harper smiled at them all and said hello to Sarah. Then she asked the girls about what was going on at the school. The twins relaxed a bit and began to tell her about some of the things they had been doing, like making cookies and getting new dresses and going to church for Easter. Mrs. Harper made pleasant comments about everything, and Sarah wondered if the girls remembered a happier Mrs. Harper.

As the girls were chatting with Mrs. Harper, Sarah heard Rachel and Miss Debbie talking about release dates and accommodations. She wondered how much time they had before Mrs. Harper returned. They only stayed about thirty minutes, and once again, Sarah noticed that Mrs. Harper was starting to look tired. As they said their good-byes and left the room, Sarah got her answer. She heard Rachel tell Miss Debbie that it would still be about a month before Mrs. Harper would be strong enough to make the move back to the school. Her plan was to accompany her friend and help out until the cast came off her leg and she was feeling stronger. Sarah breathed a little easier knowing they still had some time before everything changed again.

When the girls got back to the school, Miss Debbie said her good-byes and reminded them she would see them tomorrow for lessons. She waited till they got inside the school and waved back to her that all was well. She drove off as the twins raced inside to tell the other girls about their visit with Mrs. Harper.

When Sarah got inside, all the girls were gathered around the twins as they outlined what had happened at the center.

"Mrs. Harper looked so different," Emma told them.

"And she was nice to us," Sophie continued. The twins went on to tell the other girls all about the differences they had noticed and how kind Mrs. Harper had been to them and Sarah.

Sarah headed up the stairs with the heavy weight of confusion on her shoulders. She wondered again what it all meant. Was Mrs. Harper really changed, or would her memory all come back to her in time? Would the crotchety old Mrs. Harper return in time once she started to remember? Sarah just didn't know what to think.

The next day, Miss Debbie came for lessons. It was August now, and summer was winding down. Miss Debbie told them that she had some ideas for the new school year, but she wanted to run them by Mrs. Harper since she would be coming back to the school the first week in September. She was hoping to divide the girls into smaller groups in order to get more information to the older girls. In one large group, she spent a lot of time working with the younger girls while the older girls sat idle. If she put them in smaller groups, she could have the older girls take turns working with the younger group and have more time to spend with the rest of the girls. There would be three older groups: Olivia and the twins, Maddi, Gabbi, Katie, and Kodi and Sarah. If one of the older girls worked with Lucy and Nora, the others could all move on to more age-appropriate studies. She was hoping that Mrs. Harper's return would not cause a relapse to the old ways of running the school and thwart her plans for improving the education the girls received. She planned to fill Rachel and Mrs. Harper in on how things were currently running before their return to the school. She also wanted to talk to Mrs. Harper about letting her take Sarah along to the high school class she taught on

Tuesday and Thursday evenings, but that might have to wait until next year with everything else that was happening.

Miss Debbie kept the rest of August's lessons about games and cooking and outdoor activities. She had helped the girls plant a small garden in the late spring, and they were starting to enjoy some of the herbs and vegetables they had grown that were ready to harvest. The girls were spending a lot more time outside now, enjoying the sunshine and watering and weeding their little garden. Occasionally, they went on walks around the neighborhood too, with each of the younger girls paired with one of the older girls, while Sarah pushed little Grace in a stroller that Miss Jackie borrowed from their church. They were all going to be sad to see this particular summer come to an end. They had a huge outdoor birthday party for Olivia, who turned seven on August 23rd. They sat up folding tables outside for games and eating, and Mr. Frank brought over a grill and cooked hot dogs and hamburgers outside. The girls had never eaten outside before, so it was a rare treat! The grand finale was a huge, three-layer cake that Miss Jeannie and Miss Jackie made, covered in flowers and butterflies. Sarah had never seen Olivia so animated and happy. She had to fight down the feeling of sadness that almost overwhelmed her at the thought of Mrs. Harper's return, causing the end of all the wonderful things the girls had been able to experience in the last seven months.

12

A WEEK BEFORE MRS. Harper was due to arrive, there was a flurry of activity at the school. Some men came one day and built a temporary ramp up to the front of the building so Mrs. Harper's wheelchair could come and go more easily. An additional bed and cabinet arrived and were added to the room on the other side of the sitting room, which was outside the bedroom where Mrs. Harper stayed, so Rachel would have a place to sleep and keep a few belongings. She planned to stay at the school for as long as Mrs. Harper needed her. A visiting nurse came to check out Mrs. Harper's living arrangements and make sure all the medicines and equipment needed were in place. She would be visiting regularly once Mrs. Harper was home.

The day of Mrs. Harper's return was bright and sunny, but the girls could not shake the nervous apprehension that hung in the air. They scurried around the morning of her arrival, putting on clean clothes and making sure everything upstairs was neat and tidy. They ate breakfast solemnly in the dining room, quietly wondering if this would be the last time they were allowed to do so. They quickly cleaned up their dishes and helped Miss Jeannie and Miss Jackie clean up the kitchen. They straightened every pillow, brushed off invisible specks of dust, and made numerous trips to the windows, looking for the car that would bring Mrs. Harper home. Miss Debbie arrived shortly after breakfast and tried to reassure the girls, but no one could really predict what was going to happen. Even little Grace seemed unusually subdued, and as the car finally pulled up out front, Lucy ran to Miss Jeannie and tried to hide behind her.

The girls watched out the window as Rachel got out of the car and came around to the other side to get the wheelchair out and help Mrs. Harper into it. This was the first time many of the girls had seen her since before the accident, and Sarah heard the whispering among them about how different she looked. Mrs. Harper's hair was brushed back from her face but left down and pulled up on the sides with barrettes. After seeing her with her hair pulled up in a tight bun the whole time they had known her, seeing this softer-looking Mrs. Harper was quite a shock to most of them. Sarah knew exactly how they felt, remembering her first meeting with Mrs. Harper at the center. Soon they were at the door, and Miss Debbie was welcoming them inside.

When Mrs. Harper and her friend Rachel came inside the house, all the girls sat primly on the sofa or stood behind it, waiting for someone to speak. Miss Jeannie and Miss Jackie stood nervously in the doorway of the dining room. Miss Debbie spoke to them quietly, asking them how the drive was and telling them the girls were all ready to meet them. As Rachel wheeled Mrs. Harper into the parlor, she looked around at all the apprehensive faces and beamed!

"Hello, girls." She smiled. "It is so good to be home! I will need all of you to help me adjust to living here again as my memory is not very good since the accident, and I don't really know how things are run around here. Do you think you can all help me learn how to run the school again?" The girls looked at one another anxiously and nodded to Mrs. Harper without a word. Mrs. Harper turned toward the dining-room door next and said, "You must be Miss Jackie and Miss Jeannie. I owe you a huge thank-you for all you have done for the girls and the school in my absence!"

As Miss Jackie and Miss Jeannie came forward and shook Miss Harper's hand, Sarah marveled at how different Mrs. Harper appeared. No dark skirt and white blouse and no tight black bun. But more importantly, she sounded so *kind*! She wondered if this could be real.

"I think it would be nice if one of you could show me where Mrs. Harper's bedroom is so I can get her things settled," Rachel said next.

Maddi quickly raised her hand. "I can show you," she said quickly. "Just follow me." Maddi picked up the large bag that Rachel had set inside the door and proudly led the women toward the hallway that led to the bedroom and sitting room that Mrs. Harper had always used.

Miss Jeannie and Miss Jackie smiled at her enthusiasm but looked at the others with some concern. It was obvious that this was not the Mrs. Harper they were used to.

Miss Debbie noticed as well and gathered the girls together as Mrs. Harper and Rachel disappeared into the hallway and Maddi returned. "Let's give this a chance and see what happens, okay?" she addressed all the girls and Miss Jackie and Miss Jeannie as well. "Mrs. Harper has been very, very ill, and it may be a while before she remembers anything at all about the school. For now, she seems to remember each of you girls and has been trying hard to make sure she gets your names and circumstances correct. I have been working with her and Rachel to explain how we have been doing things since she has been gone, and Mrs. Harper seems happy to let things continue as they are. Let's just try to help her adjust to being home and getting to know everyone again, okay? This could be a great experience for all of us!"

The days turned into weeks after Mrs. Harper returned to her Heavenly Home for Girls. At first, the girls were very quiet around her, but little by little, they began to unwind and speak with her. Rachel was always right beside her, with words of encouragement for all of them. The twins still vaguely remembered this kinder woman who had cared for them early on in their father's marriage to her. The first time she referred to them as "my beautiful girls," they both looked at each other in shock! Later that night, they told the others that they remembered Mrs. Harper calling them that when their father was alive. Sarah didn't see how they could, since they were only three when she got to the school, but they seemed to believe it so she kept her thoughts to herself. Slowly they all began to believe that Mrs. Harper might not go back to being the mean, critical woman that she had been before the accident.

Maddi, with her sweet nature, had already decided that she liked the new Mrs. Harper. She offered to show her homework and shared information about what the girls had been doing in her absence. Mrs. Harper always had a ready smile for her, and Maddi would sometimes brush her hair and sing to her. Gabbi, always close by, followed Maddi's lead and often participated as well. Mrs. Harper loved her long curly hair and would often watch as Maddi put it in braids or elaborate dos.

Little Lucy and Nora had no hesitancy in letting Mrs. Harper pick them up and let them sit on her lap in the wheelchair. Often they would drag a storybook over to her, and the girls watched in disbelief as Mrs. Harper actually read it to them! Olivia, however, was tougher to win over. She had never forgotten how Mrs. Harper took their treats and yelled at Sarah. And Sarah kept her distance as well. She answered politely when Mrs. Harper spoke to her, but she preferred to talk with Rachel, who was always willing to chat with her about school and future learning possibilities. Katie and Kodi kept themselves a bit apart as well, still leery of the possibility that the old Mrs. Harper might be lurking behind her smile—and never forgetting for a moment the night she sent them all to bed with no dinner and threatened to lock them in the basement.

Miss Jeannie and Miss Jackie continued to handle meals and activities with the girls, and Mrs. Harper had actually put them on her payroll. They both appreciated the extra money, but they would have continued helping the girls for free if things had not changed. Sometimes when the girls were baking or decorating cookies, Mrs. Harper would join them. Other times she would go to her own room to read or visit with Rachel.

Miss Debbie's plan for the school year was in full swing now, and Mrs. Harper had given her permission to set it up any way she liked. As a result, Lucy and Nora were part of a preschool group while Olivia and the twins made up a first-level school group. Maddi and Gabbi and Katie and Kodi worked as a higher-level group, rotating with Sarah to lead the little ones when Miss Debbie was working with one of the other groups of girls. Miss Jeannie and Miss Jackie also helped with the preschool group, often working with them in the dining room so the other girls had more room and less distractions during study time.

And little Grace had become the darling of the school! She was often spotted playing near Mrs. Harper, and taking care of the little girl seemed to give Mrs. Harper new incentive for getting better. They seemed to be learning to walk together. Mrs. Harper had gotten her cast off and was staying out of her wheelchair most of the time now, and Grace could keep up with her slow steps. Often the girls would see Mrs. Harper and Grace walking around the living room hand in hand, slowly learning the ins and outs of maneuvering around the furniture and other obstacles. Then they would both snuggle on the couch and fall asleep, exhausted with their efforts.

13

THE FIRST WEEK OF October, the girls decided that it must be close to Grace's birthday. When they found her in January, Sarah remembered she had been wearing clothes that were marked size three months. If she was three months old in January, it meant that October would make her one year old! Since nobody knew for sure, they decided to go with the middle of the month and use October 15 as her birthday. Little Lucy would turn four on October 7, and Nora would be five on October 20, so they could have one big party for all three girls at the middle of the month! Rachel was planning to leave at the end of the month, so this way, she could be part of the celebration before she left. Miss Jackie and Miss Jeannie were pretty sure their church would host the party as they had for Sarah, so they all started writing down ideas to make it special. They couldn't wait to tell Miss Debbie their plan when she came the next day.

Mrs. Harper watched the girls as they sat around the parlor and dining room writing down fun things to do for the birthday party. How had she ever allowed herself to miss all the fun of having a bunch of girls around? She was starting to get her memory back now that she was home, but only Rachel knew. Mrs. Harper was afraid the girls would go back to hating her if she let on that she remembered what it was like before. She had been so bitter about losing one more person she loved after the twins' father had died, that she had let herself take it out on these poor, darling girls. Now she was nothing to them but a bad memory, and who could blame them? A tear slid silently down her cheek, and she quickly wiped it away before anyone could see and limped off to her bedroom. "Stop being a baby," she scolded herself. "You brought this all on yourself! You don't deserve their love!"

Miss Jackie saw Mrs. Harper hobble off to her room and couldn't help but feel a bit sorry for her. She hadn't been around to see how she had treated the girls before her accident, but she knew from the girls that it had not been good. Still she felt a bit sorry for her and wished there was something she could do.

When Miss Debbie came for lessons the next day, all the girls were waiting in a group to tell her their ideas for the birthday party. She listened intently, noticing that Mrs. Harper was leaning in the door to the dining room listening as well. Miss Jeannie piped up and said that she had checked with the church, and everyone there was very agreeable to hosting another party. Their church was happy to help and had been enjoying having the girls as part of their congregation whenever they could make it. Miss Debbie looked at all the expectant faces and turned to Mrs. Harper. "Well, Maree," she said, "what do you think?" Ten apprehensive little faces turned her way.

"I think it sounds like a wonderful idea!" she said. "There is only one stipulation that I can think of." She slowly looked around at the anxious faces before saying, "Can I come?"

Suddenly a resounding, "Yes, Yes!" filled the air as the girls all ran over to Mrs. Harper to smile at her and make her feel part of the event. Maddi took her hands and kissed them, saying happily, "We would love for you to be part of it!"

Even Sarah smiled and came over to put her arm around Mrs. Harper. "Thank you, Mrs. Harper," she whispered. To her surprise, she saw the beginning of tears in Mrs. Harper's eyes and quickly stepped away. Was Mrs. Harper really starting to like doing things with them? Maybe there was hope for this school yet!

Rachel stepped out of their sitting area where she had been working on some correspondence. "What is all the noise out here?" she said. "Aren't you supposed to be going to classes?" Although she tried to sound gruff, she couldn't hide her smile and didn't fool the girls a bit.

"Will you come too, Rachel?" Olivia questioned her. *"Please!"*

"I assume you are talking about the birthday party that all of you have been whispering about, and yes, of course, I will come! I wouldn't miss it for the world."

Rachel and Maree exchanged smiles as the girls all headed upstairs with Miss Debbie to begin their lessons. Since Miss Debbie was starting out with the twins and Olivia, she asked Kodi to take Lucy and Nora down to the dining room where Miss Jackie was going to help them with their letters. Miss Jeannie already had little Gracie, although it wasn't long before she went over to Rachel and Mrs. Harper, looking for their attention. They sat down on the floor in the parlor with her, helping her to build a tower with the building blocks that Mr. Frank had dropped off the week before.

Miss Jeannie could see that Grace was in good hands, so she went into the dining room to help Miss Jackie with Lucy and Nora. They were writing their letters with slow, concentrated effort after painstakingly putting their names on the top of the papers Miss Jackie had given them. They were progressing very well in this smaller group setting, and even Mrs. Harper could see the progress they were making.

Out of the blue, Lucy asked Miss Jackie, "Do you think Mrs. Harper is going to be mean to us again someday?"

Before Miss Jackie could answer her, Nora spoke up solemnly, "Of course not, silly! She isn't like that anymore.

Remember what Sarah said about God's grace? I think Mrs. Harper got some grace, and now she is nice. God doesn't take back His gifts, you know."

Lucy shook her head, acknowledging Nora's answer, and went on with her writing. Miss Jackie and Miss Jeannie just looked at each other in awe and smiled. *Out of the mouths of babes*, they thought.

Out in the parlor, Grace had fallen asleep, and Mrs. Harper was lying on the couch with her, stroking her hair, as Miss Rachel quietly picked up the blocks. They could hear every word the little girls were saying. Mrs. Harper looked at Rachel and raised her eyebrows. "God's grace. Hmm," she mumbled. "Maybe I better get out my own Bible."

14

THE DAYS AND WEEKS flew by, and soon it was only a couple of days before the party. The girls had made cards for each of the little ones, and everyone was talking about the church and the bus and remembering everything that had happened for Sarah's party. They had made adorable little crowns for Grace, Lucy, and Nora and covered them in foil to make them shine. They were trying to decide what the little girls should wear to the party at breakfast one morning when Mrs. Harper walked in and sat down with them. Miss Jeannie handed her a cup of coffee and asked if she would like a muffin. She thanked her and bit into the delicious blueberry muffin, knowing the girls had all helped to make them the day before. "Wow," she said. "These muffins are amazing!"

"We helped make them," Olivia said in a solemn tone. "Do you really like them, Mrs. Harper?"

"Of course, I do, sweetie. They are very good." Olivia smiled at Mrs. Harper for the first time that Sarah could remember. "And by the way," continued Mrs. Harper, looking around at all the girls, "do you think you could all call me Miss Maree, like you do Miss Debbie? Mrs. Harper sounds kind of grouchy, don't you think?"

Some of the younger girls giggled, and the rest of the girls smiled. "Miss Maree," said Olivia quietly, "I like that!"

Miss Maree just smiled and reached over and patted Olivia's hand as she finished her muffin. *Maybe there is hope after all*, Miss Maree thought. *Maybe this really can be the Heavenly Home for Girls that I've always wanted.* She had been reading her Bible since overhearing Nora's comments about God's grace, and she was starting to believe that life was not so bad, after all. Looking at all the happy faces around the table made it even easier.

After breakfast, Miss Maree pulled Sarah aside and asked her about gifts for the little girls for their birthdays. She wondered if Sarah would go with her and Rachel to help pick something out for each of them. Having heard the conversation about what the girls should wear to the party, she wondered if she might buy each of them something new to wear as well. Sarah beamed at Miss Maree and told her she would love to go, even though it wasn't really necessary. Rachel walked up at that moment and told her that birthdays weren't about what was necessary. She encouraged Sarah to check on the girls and get her things so they could leave in about twenty minutes. Miss Jackie, overhearing the whole conversation, told Sarah that she would be happy to play a game or two with the girls while Sarah was gone. Sarah almost skipped up the stairs, hardly believing this wondrous turn of events.

Rachel and Miss Maree were already in the car when Sarah came back downstairs with the girls, and Miss Jackie was ready and waiting for them. She had games arranged on the dining-room table for the girls and a high chair with little baby snacks all ready for Grace. Sarah slipped out the door and got into the backseat before the girls even knew she was gone.

To Sarah's amazement, Rachel drove them directly to the mall. Sarah had never been there before and looked around at all the stores, wondering if she had died and gone to heaven. Sensing her awe, Miss Maree took her time making her way around, giving Sarah time to take it all in. She told Sarah she would like to head to Macy's department store as she knew they were having a sale in their children's department and hoped they could find something there for all three of the little girls. When they got to Macy's, they headed to the escalator and started up to the third floor where the children's department was located. Sarah held on tight to the railing, feeling silly and apprehensive and excited all at once. Soon they were looking around at racks and racks of children's clothing, shoes, stuffed animals, and toys.

After they had walked around for a bit, Rachel spotted a soft pink outfit that had tiny rosebuds around the neck and hem of the top and supersoft leggings with ruffles. It came with a mint-green sweater that matched the stems of the rosebuds and was as soft as a cloud. Little ballet slippers completed the outfit, along with a tiny headband of rosebuds.

"Oh, it's perfect," Sarah exclaimed. "But is it too much?" She looked nervously at Miss Maree.

"Of course, it isn't!" Miss Maree stated. "Everything in the department is 50 percent off today, so I am not even looking at prices. Today is about what you think they would like and nothing else." She smiled at Sarah to soften the words, and Sarah smiled back. Miss Maree held up a little baby doll in its own little basket, and Sarah nodded enthusiastically. "One down, two to go," Miss Maree said.

As they went on looking for outfits for Lucy and Nora, Sarah thought she had never had so much fun! They picked out a pale-teal velvet jumper for Lucy with the softest little blouse and matching tights. They topped it off with stretchy little Mary Jane–style slippers and a matching teal bow for her hair. They got her an interactive storybook, which actually read the story aloud and let you follow along with the words! Sarah knew she would love it! And for Nora, they found the cutest purple tunic and leggings in the softest material that Sarah had ever touched. It had white fluff around the neck and sleeves with a little white muff for your hands that Sarah knew Nora would adore. Miss Maree insisted on buying the little boots that matched the outfit. They picked out an art set for Nora (who was always drawing) with colored pencils, crayons, paints, and more. Sarah could not wait for the girls to open all the wonderful presents.

As they finished up their final purchases and waited for the saleslady to wrap everything up, Miss Maree suggested they go into the coffee shop for something to drink. Rachel agreed and said she was extremely thirsty, so they made their way to the back of the store and sat in a comfy leather booth. When the waitress came to take their order, Miss Maree ordered a flavored iced tea, and Rachel asked for a raspberry smoothie. Sarah had no idea what to order, so Rachel told her all the smoothie flavors, and Sarah decided on a peach-mango smoothie. It was delicious!

They finished their drinks and picked up their packages. Rachel suggested she run the packages out to the car since it was nearby. Miss Maree turned to Sarah and told her that she wanted to get her an outfit as well since she knew Sarah was growing and needed a few things.

"I know I wasn't kind to you in the past," Miss Maree started, "and I want to make up for it. I know how much you do for all the girls, always putting them first and making sure they have what they need. And I'm sorry, Sarah, for every mean thing I ever did or said. I want to be different, and I want to take care of you all and make sure our school is a wonderful place to be. That's why I named it the Heavenly Home for Girls in the first place!"

Once again, Sarah saw the tears beginning in Miss Maree's eyes and knew she was being sincere. "It's okay," she started, but Miss Maree interrupted her.

"No, it isn't. But it is going to get better, I promise."

Miss Rachel walked up at that moment, and they headed out into the mall. They went to a shoe store where Miss Maree insisted that Sarah be fitted for both shoes and boots. Then they stopped at one of the popular teenage stores where Sarah tried on the softest jeans imaginable and a pretty pink shirt and matching zip-up sweatshirt. They even found pretty underwear and socks, although Sarah turned bright red when Rachel had to help her find her sizes. Sarah was getting upset about what all this was costing when Miss Maree walked up with a one-piece pajama that she insisted Sarah had to have. Finally, they checked out of the store, with Rachel and Sarah each carrying a large shopping bag and headed toward the parking lot.

They were all tired after the shopping, so it was quiet on the way home. Rachel mentioned that she had picked up little stuffed animals for all the girls on her way out to the car the first time, so everyone had a little something as a surprise. Sarah sat in the backseat and marveled at her experience, praying that it was all for real and she wasn't just dreaming! When they got back, all the girls were anticipating their return. Miss Rachel passed around the adorable little stuffed animals, even surprising Sarah with one herself. The little girls got to open their new outfits, and everyone admired them again. Sarah suggested they save the other packages for the birthday party.

After all the girls finished admiring the new outfits and Sarah had taken her own goodies upstairs, Miss Jeannie suggested they watch the Discovery Channel as there was a show on koala bears that they all wanted to see. She had popcorn and apples all ready, and the girls all ran upstairs and brought down their blankets and new stuffed animals to snuggle with. Even Sarah tucked her little stuffed panda into her blanket as she sat on the floor, leaning up against the couch with Grace on her lap and the twins on either side. Olivia, Lucy, and Nora snuggled on the couch with Miss Maree and Rachel while Miss Jeannie and Miss Jackie each took one of the stuffed chairs for their aching bones. Maddi and Gabbi leaned against Miss Jackie's chair, and Katie and Kodi leaned against Miss Jeannie's chair. Everyone had small cups of popcorn and crispy apples to munch as they watched the show that explained all about koala bears— where they lived, what they ate, and everything about their natural habitat. They looked like one big happy family!

15

THE DAY OF THE birthday party was beautiful, with blue skies and sunshine. It was a typical Indian-summer day, a bit warmer than most October weather. It was Saturday, and the church bus was going to arrive at noon as the church ladies were planning to serve the girls lunch this time. The girls had been so excited at breakfast that they had hurried through eating and cleanup in order to rush upstairs to figure out what they were wearing to the party.

During Mr. Frank's last trip to the school, he and a friend had hauled a large wardrobe upstairs for the girls that had five drawers on each side and a large space in the middle for hanging clothes. It gave each of the girls another drawer for clothing and also allowed their dresses and jackets to be hung in the center. Mr. Frank's wife had made pretty labels for each of the girls to put on their individual drawers, which helped everyone to be more organized. Now Sarah watched the girls as they jostled one another in their efforts to get what they wanted to wear out of the wardrobe.

Sarah was wearing her new jeans and pretty pink shirt and had knotted the matching sweatshirt around her waist. She had laid Grace's, Lucy's, and Nora's outfits on her bed in preparation for helping the little ones into their special birthday finery and was just thinking about starting the process as Tahler and Destani came up the stairs to help. Miss Debbie had joined the girls for breakfast, and Miss Jill and Miss Becky had arrived right after, bringing their granddaughters who were excited to help the little girls get ready for their big day! The girls were all happy to see them again and chattered nonstop with them as everyone began getting ready. Maddi had finished special "hairdos" for Lucy and Nora earlier and reminded the girls not to mess them up as they got ready. She was wearing skinny little jeans and a long sweater herself and looked adorable as she went from girl to girl to see if anyone needed help with their hair. With the extra help from Tahler and Destani, they were ready in record time. Soon they were lined up and heading downstairs to wait for the bus.

Miss Maree and Rachel were waiting for the girls below and had been visiting with Miss Debbie's sisters while they waited for the girls. They smiled and complimented the girls as they came downstairs, with Miss Becky immediately reaching for Grace and giving her a big hug! Sarah was smiling in pride at all the girls when she noticed the concerned look on Katie's face and realized that Kodi was not at her side as usual. When she walked over to

Katie, Katie whispered something in her ear. Sarah told Miss Debbie that she would be right back and hurried back upstairs to find Kodi huddled on her bed, crying. Although Kodi was almost as big as Sarah, she was still a couple of years younger. She put her arms around Kodi, trying to determine the cause of her tears.

"M-my pants are just too tight," Kodi sobbed. "And I have nothing nice to wear!"

Sarah had Kodi stand up so she could take a look. Sure enough, the pants were too short, and Kodi could hardly button them. "Hey," Sarah said quietly, "how would you like to borrow the outfit I got for my birthday? You are almost as tall as I am. The pants are leggings, so they should fit you just fine. Do you want to see if they fit?"

Kodi nodded through her tears, and Sarah quickly got the outfit from her own drawer. The stretchy fabric fit Kodi just fine, and Sarah was able to cuff the sleeves on the tunic so they would not be too long.

Kodi was excited to be wearing something that fit better, so she dried her eyes and gave Sarah a hug. "Thank you, Sarah. I love it, and I will be very careful not to get it dirty."

Sarah patted her on the back and told her not to worry as they hurried downstairs to join the others. In all the excitement over the party, their absence wasn't questioned, and Sarah heard Tahler tell Kodi how nice she looked. Kodi beamed and looked over at Sarah, who gave her a thumbs-up. *Catastrophe avoided*, Sarah thought to herself.

She needed to go over clothing with the older girls and see who needed what. But for now, it was time for the party!

Soon they heard the church bus pull up out front, and everyone pulled on jackets and got ready to go. Miss Maree and Rachel were going to follow in their car as it would be a little easier for Miss Maree to get in and out of. As they walked out the front door, the bus doors swished open, and Miss Kathy was beaming hello to all of them. Everyone was familiar with the bus now, and all the little ones had someone to help them in their car seats and sit with them during the ride. Once again, Sarah found herself just one of the girls as the adults took on the responsibility of the little ones. It was a nice break, and it gave Sarah a chance to chat with Tahler again. Within minutes, they were off, headed for their second birthday party this year!

When they arrived at the church, they were led to the back door and entered as they had for Sarah's party. Soon they were inside, and everyone was greeting them and helping the little ones with their jackets. Miss Jackie and Miss Jeannie had gone over right after breakfast to help with preparations, and they came out of the kitchen to introduce the other ladies who were helping out. The girls were talking and laughing as they took their seats at the familiar table. There was a high chair for Grace and booster seats for Lucy and Nora. Sarah carefully got out the crowns they had made for the little girls, and Miss Debbie and Tahler helped her use bobby pins to attach them to their hair. They were careful not to mess up Maddi's hairdos, and soon the three little girls all wore their birthday crowns proudly!

The church ladies had set up a second table for Miss Maree, Rachel, Miss Debbie, Miss Jill, and Miss Becky right next to the one for the girls, but Tahler and Destani sat at the girls' table just in case anyone needed a hand. It was great fun, and soon the ladies were bringing out the lunch. There were platters of little sandwiches (with the crust cut off), with everything from ham and cheese to peanut butter and jelly. There were three different soups, cut-up fruits and veggies, and mini blueberry muffins. The girls all had glasses of milk to drink, with the option of adding strawberry or chocolate powder to flavor it. Lucy just loved the strawberry milk while Nora opted for chocolate.

After lunch, the ladies brought out three little cakes, one decorated for each of the birthday girls, and they all sang happy birthday and helped the little ones blow out their candles. There were cupcakes for the other girls and ice-cream cups for all. They played games and won prizes, and each of the girls had remembered their bags with their names on them for their prizes. They gave Grace and Lucy and Nora the cards they had made them, and the girls were surprised to see that even Rachel and Miss Maree had made them cards to go with their gifts. The little girls squealed when they saw their gifts from Miss Maree, and each of them got big teddy bears from the ladies at the church, along with brand-new pajamas!

All too soon, it was all over and time to get back on the bus to go home. The girls all said thank-you, and hugs were exchanged as they said their good-byes. The trip home was full of laughter and songs. Maddi and Tahler kept starting silly songs like "Row, row, row your boat" and "Old McDonald's Farm." Soon everyone was joining in the fun!

When they got back to the school, the little birthday princesses were all exhausted! Miss Debbie and Sarah helped them upstairs to take a little nap while the others gathered in the parlor with Miss Maree and Rachel. Miss Jeannie and Miss Jackie had stayed back at the church to help put everything back in order. Once again, Miss Maree surprised the girls by asking them if they would like to watch a movie that she and Rachel had picked up on their way home. It was one of her favorites, *Little Women*, and the girls were all excited to see it. They all sat on the floor in front of the sofa as Miss Jill and Miss Becky and their granddaughters cuddled on the sofa, and Miss Maree and Rachel used the chairs. As Sarah came downstairs, she handed each of the girls their blankets and stuffed animals, which she had thoughtfully gathered from their beds. Miss Debbie had offered to stay upstairs with the little ones so Sarah could go down and watch the movie with the others. Soon they were all settled down and enjoying the movie.

16

RACHEL LEFT AT THE end of the month, and the girls were very sad to see her go. On her last day, she gathered all the girls together in the parlor after breakfast. She went into her room and came back out pushing a very large box into the room. It was wrapped in bright-colored paper with silver stars. She beamed as she told all the girls that she had gotten them a going-away present, and they were all to tear off the paper and see what was inside. The girls gathered around the box in excitement, and even Grace toddled over to help. Soon paper was flying everywhere, and they were all looking at a large cardboard box. Rachel came over and helped them open it up. Inside the box were stacks of—more boxes! But each of these boxes had a name on it. Rachel asked all the girls to sit down as she passed around boxes to each of the girls. Finally, when even Grace was sitting on the floor with a box on her lap, Rachel told the girls to open their boxes!

Suddenly the room was filled with happy exclamations as each girl opened her box to find a brand-new outfit in her size! Each of the girls had a new dress or tunic with leggings that was in her favorite style or color. Sarah's attempt to pass down clothes and try to make sure all the girls had something suitable to wear to church each Sunday had not gone unnoticed. As Sarah looked around at all the girls, she almost cried! She held up her own soft-blue sweaterdress and marveled at the matching tights. All the girls were trying to get her attention, and finally Rachel said she had a great idea. They would have a fashion show before she left, and each of the girls would come out wearing her new outfit and walking around so everyone could see it. The girls thought it was a wonderful idea and hurried upstairs to get ready! Miss Jeannie and Miss Jackie went up with the girls to help with the little ones, and soon they were all back downstairs in their new outfits. Rachel stood up and announced each girl, starting with Sarah. As the girls stood up and started around the room so everyone could see their outfit, Rachel described the outfit like they do at a fashion show.

"This is our lovely Sarah," she started. "Notice how the blue sweaterdress matches the blue of her eyes, and please notice that her tights look like they were made to go with the dress. Please give Sarah a hand," Rachel finished as Sarah finished her walk and sat back down. The girls clapped wildly after each girl walked around the room. Finally, it was down to little Grace.

"And now for the finale, we have our cute little baby doll, Grace. Please pay attention to her headband and tights, which bring out the dark purple in her soft flannel maxi dress. Also note the little black boots that compliment her outfit. Such a cute little fashion bug!" The girls all clapped for Grace, who suddenly (without coaxing from anyone) did a deep curtsy and sat back down. Miss Maree and Miss Jackie and Miss Jeannie declared the fashion show a success! All the girls hurried back upstairs to take care of their new clothes and change back to their playclothes. Once they were all changed, they filed back downstairs to thank Rachel again and say their final good-byes. Rachel promised to return for movie nights now and then and told the girls Miss Maree would keep her up to date on what was happening at the school. Miss Maree reassured the girls that nothing was really changing that much. Still, the girls worried that once Rachel was gone, the old Mrs. Harper might return. They could not quite believe that Miss Maree was here to stay. At least tomorrow was Sunday, which meant they would get to go to church and wear the special outfits that Rachel had given them. Miss Jeannie and Miss Jackie were still with them too, and that gave them another bit of comfort.

That night, Sarah could sense the unease among the girls, so she decided to get out her trusty Bible and read a story. It always calmed the girls and made Sarah feel good as well. As the girls got into their pajamas, Sarah searched in her Bible for a story that might make the girls feel better about the future. She found a story in Timothy 2 titled "Encouragement to be Faithful" and decided to use this story to try to remind the girls to stop fretting and pray for strength through God's grace. As the girls climbed into bed, they saw the Bible on Sarah's bed and knew it was time for one of her stories. They snuggled down and waited in anticipation. Sarah started out by saying that many things in life were difficult at times and hard to understand. She mentioned Rachel leaving and the uncertainty of change and everyone's worry that someday the old Mrs. Harper would return. She looked around the room at all the little faces listening with rapt attention. Finally, she asked the girls if they had any ideas about what they could do to get rid of some of the fears they were feeling.

Sophie was the first one to raise her hand, and Sarah picked her to start the discussion. "I think we should pray about it," she said softly. "Maybe God can keep Miss Maree from remembering to be mean old Mrs. Harper!"

Of course, her twin, Emma, had something to add, "I think I remember Miss Maree when she was married to Daddy and loved us. I am going to pray for her to stay the way she is! I think she just forgot how to be nice before." Sophie looked at Emma and nodded her agreement.

"Well, I think you girls are on the right track," Sarah said with approval. "Praying to God is always a good way to gain strength." Looking over at little Grace, who was sound asleep in her crib, she continued, "Remember when we named baby Grace? Can anyone tell me why we chose that name?"

Gabbi's hand flew into the air, and before Sarah could call on her, she said, "She was our little gift from God, because if we believe in God, He provides us His grace. God knew we would take care of her, so He gave her to us to love."

Sarah was amazed at how smart the girls were and how much they remembered. It made sharing her Bible with them so rewarding. "You are right, Gabbi! God trusted us to love and take care of Grace, and He gave us the strength to do it." Looking down at her Bible, she read, "'God's grace is the means by which God makes Himself everything we need to utterly abound.' If we believe in God, He will give us the strength we need to handle every challenge, every need, every conflict we encounter. God's grace is unlimited, and it says in 2 Timothy 2:1, 'You then, my son (or daughter), be strong, in the grace that is in Christ Jesus.' So very simply, God's grace is our strength!"

Sarah looked around again, sensing a feeling of understanding and relief. She closed her Bible and told the girls that their strength to handle whatever happened with Miss Maree lay in the power of their prayers and God's gift of grace as a result. Sarah suggested that they all pray together to make sure that God knew they were counting on His guidance in the days to come. They stretched out their hands, from bed to bed and girl to girl, even holding the sides of Gracie's crib so that she would be included in the circle of prayer. As they bowed their heads in unison, Sarah prayed, "Heavenly Father, hear our prayers and know that we are all counting on You to give us the strength we need in the coming days and weeks and months. We believe in You, God, and in Your Son, Jesus Christ. We know that only *You* can get us through the challenges and conflicts that we face, and we ask for Your continued grace in our lives. Thank You for all our blessings and please continue to heal Miss Maree and keep her nice. Amen."

As the girls settled down for the night, a feeling of peace settled over the room. Even the woman who stood quietly listening at the top of the stairs felt it. And as Miss Maree made her way quietly back downstairs and into her bedroom—as she got out her Bible and read 2 Timothy 2:1—tears slid silently down her cheeks.

17

THE FIRST COUPLE OF weeks of November came and went. The girls settled into their routine of classes on Monday, Wednesday, and Friday afternoons and laundry on Thursday. But now, in addition to those things, there were Friday movie nights and Sundays at church. Miss Maree was part of everything now, only going into her office for a couple of hours in the morning after breakfast or during the afternoon, if the girls were all busy with lessons. And the girls were welcome to come and go downstairs most of the time, as long as Sarah or Miss Jeannie or Miss Jackie was aware of what they were doing. Grace had begun to follow Miss Maree everywhere, and often the girls would see Miss Maree take Grace's high chair into her office so she could have a snack close by while Miss Maree was working. The Heavenly Home for Girls was a happy place to be.

Child Protective Services still checked in regularly with the school, and occasionally they would send prospective foster parents or people interested in adopting over to meet the girls. This made the girls tense and worried, fearing that one or more of them might have to leave. They all knew that little Grace was the one most likely to be chosen, and they wondered how Miss Maree would feel if someone wanted to take her. And all the girls, especially Sarah, would be devastated!

One couple in particular seemed very interested in little Grace. When they returned for a second time the week of Thanksgiving and went into Miss Maree's office, everyone was afraid they would take her away. All the girls sat in the parlor with Miss Jeannie and Miss Jackie, anxiously waiting to see what would happen when they came out. Thankfully, Grace was fast asleep on the couch, unaware of all the hovering girls. Finally, the door to Miss Maree's office opened, and the disappointed-looking couple left. A beaming Miss Maree walked into the parlor with a smile on her face. "Why all the long faces?" she asked the girls.

Maddi stood up quickly and said what all the girls were thinking, "We thought they were going to take Grace!"

Miss Maree looked around the room at all the faces who had become dear to her and said reassuringly, "Why would they do that when I have adopted her?" The girls all gathered around her, talking at once. "Shhhh," Miss Maree cautioned, "Grace is still sleeping!" She walked over to the sleeping toddler and tucked a stray curl behind her ear. "She belongs to all of us now." The girls watched in wonder as Miss Jeannie and Miss Jackie gave Miss Maree a hug, expressing their thanks as well. And as Sarah watched it all unfold, she said her own little prayer to God. Amazing Grace indeed!

As Thanksgiving neared, the girls felt the excitement of planning for a holiday gathering. Turkey pictures were made and displayed throughout the house, and every day new treats were baked and decorated for the big day. Miss Debbie was coming for dinner, and an additional table and chairs had been purchased to accommodate everyone, including all the adults. It was going to be a fun and festive day!

When the girls awoke on Thanksgiving morning, wonderful aromas filled the air! There were hot cinnamon rolls for breakfast with thick, crisp bacon and fresh fruit. The smell of turkey and stuffing was already starting to float out of the kitchen, and there were four pies already baked and setting on the counter. Miss Jeannie asked for volunteers to peel the mountain of potatoes, and Sarah and Katie and Kodi offered to help. Soon they were all crowding around the sink, peeling and rinsing the potatoes and placing them in a large pot for boiling. Miss Jackie was reading a holiday story about the first Thanksgiving to the rest of the girls, keeping it loud enough so the girls in the kitchen could hear it as well. Once the story and potatoes were finished, Miss Maree turned on the Thanksgiving Day parade for all the girls to watch. She had purchased a very large flat television that Mr. Frank had mounted on the wall of the parlor. It had a beautiful picture and was big enough that everyone in the room could see it. No more crowding around the rickety old television set. She had also added another couch and colorful beanbags to the room to make it more comfortable for the girls. It had become their favorite room in the house!

Miss Debbie arrived during the parade, bringing warm homemade rolls and her special cranberry sauce. Soon she joined Sarah, Katie, and Kodi on the couch while Miss Jackie and Miss Jeannie took a break from the kitchen to watch some of the parade with them. The girls oohed and ahhed in appreciation of the bands and floats and singing. It was the first time any of them had seen the Thanksgiving Day parade.

Dinner was amazing, with turkey and stuffing, mashed potatoes and gravy, squash and corn, and the homemade rolls and cranberry sauce. The girls had fun eating and chatting, and Miss Maree thought she had not been this happy in a long, long time. She finally had the girls' school that she had planned all those years ago back in college, right down to Miss Debbie being their teacher. Miss Maree and Miss Debbie shared a look at one point during the meal, and Miss Maree knew that she was thinking along similar lines. After dinner, everyone was too full for dessert, so they decided to watch a movie while Grace had a nap. Miss Jackie took Grace to the playpen that had been purchased and set up in a distant corner of the parlor several days earlier. It made it much easier for them to keep an eye on her when she was napping. Once Grace was asleep, Miss Jackie came back and settled down to watch the movie with the girls. Lucy and Nora both fell asleep on their beanbags before the movie was over.

As the movie ended, the doorbell rang, and Mr. Frank was standing there with a huge fruit basket for all of them. Miss Maree invited him in to share a piece of pie as they all sat down to have dessert. They all laughed and talked and had a very good time. Even Grace managed a small piece of pumpkin pie with whipped cream, although there was more of the whipped cream on her face than in her mouth. Sarah looked around the happy gathering and thought this was the best time they had ever had at the Heavenly Home for Girls.

18

DECEMBER BROUGHT SNOWSTORMS THAT kept the girls inside for days. After a full week of snow, the girls were surprised by another visit from Miss Jeannie and Miss Jackie's friends from church. The girls were now familiar with Miss Nita and Miss Karen, who had both been involved in providing Easter dresses and jackets for the girls. They had also both been involved in the birthday parties at the church. After visiting for a few moments, Miss Nita went back to the car and brought in two huge shopping bags, returning for additional bags after dropping the first load off. When she finally closed the door and took off her coat and gloves, she had a big surprise for the girls. The bags were filled with coats, snow pants, boots, hats, scarves, and mittens! The girls squealed in delight as they each got fitted with outside gear. After a few switches, each girl had a full set of snow gear. Miss Maree suddenly came out of her bedroom dressed in coat, boots, hat, scarf, and mittens. When the girls looked up at her in surprise, she said, "Who wants to go outside and play?"

Katie, who had been somewhat reserved about Miss Maree up to this point, ran over and gave her a big hug. "Thank you so much, Miss Maree," she offered. "Do you really want to go outside with us? Will your leg be okay?"

"Of course, I do," Miss Maree replied. "I love the snow! My leg needs the exercise." Her comments were news to the girls, but with everyone outfitted to play in the snow, nobody was going to argue.

Miss Nita and Miss Karen put their outside gear back on, and away they all went out the door. Soon the girls were playing in the snow, throwing snowballs and making snow angels. The front lawn at the Heavenly Home for Girls had never seen this much activity. With the help of the grown-ups, a large snowman began to take shape. Once the head was placed on top of the body, Miss Maree helped the girls look for sticks and stones to use for arms and eyes and a mouth. In the nick of time (since she had been watching from the window), Miss Jeannie came outside with a big carrot to use for a nose and an old hat and scarf to place on the snowman. The girls danced around in glee at their creation, until Miss Maree declared their snow day a success and suggested they all go back in for hot cocoa and cookies.

Eleven chilly, wet girls trooped inside, with the church ladies helping them brush off the snow and get out of coats and snow pants, boots, and mittens. Miss Jackie took all the outerwear into the laundry room, putting some of it right in the dryer and draping the rest around the room to dry. In the meantime, Miss Jeannie had mugs of warm hot cocoa with marshmallows and a large platter of cookies waiting on the table in the dining room. As Sarah sat holding Gracie on her lap and helping her sip her little mug of cocoa, she smiled at the rosy cheeks and happy expressions of all the girls sitting around the table.

On Monday, when she came for lessons, Miss Debbie suggested that they should start planning for Christmas. She had spoken with Miss Maree and received permission for all the girls to attend Santa's Secret Workshop at their church. This meant that the girls would have the opportunity to buy small gifts for one another. At first, the room was filled with excited whispers and eager questions about the outing, but suddenly Sarah said very quietly, "How will we all get money to use at the workshop?"

"Well, that is the best part," Miss Debbie replied. "Miss Maree has made a list of chores that need to be completed around the house and the amount she is willing to pay for them. Each of you will be able to sign up to complete the chores and earn Christmas money. In addition, there is going to be a holiday craft show at the church, and each girl who is willing to help make popcorn, baked goods, or crafts will get to keep a small portion of the profits. The only catch is that the craft show is only ten days away, so we don't have a lot of time."

Now that a means of earning money had been outlined for the girls, the level of excitement rose. Miss Debbie passed around the list of chores, and the girls took turns signing their names to particular chores. The older girls helped the little ones sign up for the easier chores and made sure every girl had a chance to sign up for at least one chore—except for Grace, of course. She was still a bit young to understand Christmas and all the details. Miss Maree had been very generous with what she was willing to pay, so everyone would have a chance to earn some money.

Miss Debbie passed around envelopes so each girl could put their name on an envelope and save it in their drawer to hold their earnings. As Miss Debbie went on with lessons that afternoon, she could almost taste the air of excitement. The girls worked extra hard to complete their lessons quickly so they could get downstairs to talk to Miss Jackie and Miss Jeannie about their ideas for the craft show. Miss Debbie just smiled as she looked at all the happy faces, as did Miss Maree, who had been watching from her spot at the top of the stairs.

That evening, after supper, the girls approached Miss Maree, Miss Jackie, and Miss Jeannie about the craft show. They had gotten together and made a list (with Sarah's help) of the things they thought they could sell. The list contained the following items: red and green popcorn balls, hard flavored candies in little jars (using all of the empty jars that had been saved from Grace's baby-food days), snowman cookies, and pot holders. Mr. Frank had given them a pot-holder maker when he had stopped by one day and a huge bag of loops for making them. The twins had made several pot holders for Miss Jackie and Miss Jeannie, but if they all joined in and started making them daily, they would have a lot to sell. As Miss Maree, Miss Jeannie, and Miss Jackie looked over the list, the girls waited anxiously to see what the response would be. They watched as Miss Maree whispered something to Miss Jackie and Miss Jeannie, and they nodded solemnly.

Suddenly Miss Maree addressed them all. "We think it will work," she said very seriously. "But everyone is going to have to help!" The girls clapped with excitement and promised to work hard, starting with pot-holder-making that very night!

The next ten days were a flurry of activity. After meals, the girls got busy with their respective responsibilities. While a couple of the girls worked on washing windows and dusting shelves, others sat at the dining-room table making pot holders or peeling labels off baby-food jars. They also went through old boxes that Miss Maree pulled out of the attic, gathering ribbons and cutting them in lengths that they could tie around the tops of the baby-food jars or use to tie up the bags of popcorn balls. Miss Jackie and Miss Jeannie set aside the next Tuesday and Thursday and Saturday to work on the candy, popcorn balls, and cookies, making sure they didn't interfere with lessons. Sarah took on the responsibility of figuring out what each of the crafts would gain the girls, knowing that they would have to split the profit at least ten ways. The girls had counted fifty-seven baby-food jars in all, so if they filled them with hard candy and sold them for $2 each, they could make $114 dollars on the jars alone! They hoped to make at least fifty pot holders and sell them for $1 each, so that would be another $50. Depending on the number of popcorn balls and snowman cookies, she figured they should easily reach at least the $200 mark, maybe more. It was pretty exciting to think that they might have as much as $20 each to spend on Christmas gifts!

19

THE DAYS FLEW BY as the girls all worked feverishly on earning money for Santa's Secret Workshop. The pile of pot holders grew taller, and rows of clean, shining baby-food jars lined the counter in the kitchen. The only downside for Sarah was a feeling of unease she experienced as she came upstairs one evening to find Katie and Kodi quickly shutting the drawer where she kept her Bible and acting a bit strange about what they had been doing upstairs. They told her they were working on something for Miss Debbie, but Sarah could see they were both uncomfortable. The next day, she checked her drawer, but she could not find anything out of place or missing, so she put it out of her mind.

On Thursday, the girls finished their laundry as quickly as they could after breakfast. In the afternoon, they were going to make the hard candy that would go in the baby-food jars. Miss Jackie was heading this up and had several colors and flavors for the girls to pick from as they gathered in the dining room that afternoon. She explained that she would be cooking the sugar mixture then adding the color and flavoring before she placed it on cookie sheets to harden. Once it had hardened, the girls would break it into pieces and place it in the prepared jars. She brought out a cookie sheet with candy that had already been prepared to show them what she meant. She brought out a very small hammer that they would use to crack the candy. It was red and shiny, and Miss Jackie told them it was cherry flavor. She took the hammer and carefully struck the candy on the cookie sheet in several places. The candy cracked in every direction, making tiny pieces of hard candy in every shape imaginable.

Miss Jackie showed them how to put on little plastic gloves and pick up the pieces, carefully placing a few in each jar. They would repeat this process with other colors and flavors of candy. The girls took turns smelling the different flavors, finally settling on lime with green coloring, pineapple with yellow coloring, and grape with purple coloring. Miss Jackie thought they would go well with the red cherry candy that was already made. As Miss Jackie returned to the kitchen to make the next color of candy, Sarah helped the girls put on gloves and get the red candy into the jars. By the time they had finished, Miss Jackie had another color ready to crack and put in the jars with the other pieces.

Miss Maree stopped in to watch their efforts and provide praise, and noticing that Gracie was becoming a distraction for Sarah, she took the little girl off for a story. Once the girls got all four colors in the jars, they began the process of tying the ribbons that they had sorted and cut around the tops of the jars. As the rows of jars grew, the girls looked at them in awe! Row after row of pretty, colorful little jars of candy—fifty-seven in all, and they were perfect! The girls ran to the kitchen to hug Miss Jackie and Miss Jeannie, who had pitched in when things got a bit hectic at the stove. Miss Jackie was sweaty and sticky all over, but she was happy to help the girls and thrilled when they insisted that both ladies keep one of the little jars for themselves!

On Friday, Miss Debbie came for lessons and separated the girls into their usual groups. It was Sarah's turn to help with the little ones, so she headed downstairs with them to use the dining room, knowing that Miss Jackie and Miss Jeannie would work with Lucy and Nora while she focused on Olivia and the twins. As soon as she left, Miss Debbie turned to Katie and Kodi, asking them how things were going. Katie explained that they were doing okay and showed Miss Debbie what they had accomplished so far. She was pleased and suggested she take the completed ones with her. She gave them more paper and showed Maddi and Gabbi what they were trying to do. The two girls picked up on it quickly, and soon they were all working diligently, using Sarah's Bible that Katie had carefully taken out of Sarah's drawer. Katie mentioned that Sarah had almost caught her and Kodi using it one day, but they didn't think

Sarah was mad about it so far. Miss Debbie told them to be more careful, especially now that all four of them could work on them. She suggested they determine small periods of time when two of them could come upstairs without alerting Sarah. Miss Debbie collected all the ones they completed during lessons and planned to take them with her to be laminated. Then they went on with a lesson so Sarah would not be suspicious if she returned with the other girls.

Saturday was cookie day! The girls quickly cleaned up the dishes after breakfast, carrying them into the kitchen to be loaded into the dishwasher. Once that was done, Miss Jeannie got out a folding table that the girls could gather around while they were rolling out the dough and cutting the cookies. Miss Jackie stood by with a cookie sheet so the girls could place them on it as soon as they cut out a snowman. She slid the cookie sheet into the oven and stood ready with a fresh cookie sheet for the next batch of snowmen. By the time one sheet came out golden brown, another sheet was ready to pop in the oven. Before long, the girls had stacks and stacks of snowmen ready to decorate. Miss Jeannie carried the bowls of cookies into the dining room and placed the snowy-white frosting that she had made earlier around the table. The girls each had their own butter knife to spread the yummy buttercream frosting onto the snowmen cookies.

Miss Maree was as excited as the girls as she helped Grace frost her first snowman. They pressed on mini M&M's for the eyes and mouth and tiny little orange noses that Miss Jeannie had made out of orange gumdrops. Miss Jackie and Miss Jeannie had also created a variety of candy hats and scarfs, and placing them on the snowmen was almost like dressing paper dolls! Sarah declared her first snowman a "snow woman" with its purple hat and scarf, and soon the girls were all competing to see who could create the best snowman.

After a while, Nora and Lucy got tired and left the table to watch a movie with Miss Maree and Grace; and shortly afterward, the twins followed suit. Surprisingly, it was little Olivia who had a knack for creating the nicest snowmen, and she worked tirelessly until every cookie was frosted and decorated. She received high praise for the number of cookies she finished and was declared the "best cookie decorator" by all the other girls. Sarah looked at the table covered in colorful snowmen and thought the girls had done a fantastic job. As she counted the snowmen, she realized that they had created about five dozen cookies or sixty snowmen. If they sold each one for $1, that was another $60 to add to their total!

At church Sunday, the announcements included mention of both the craft show on Thursday and Santa's Secret Workshop on Saturday! The girls could hardly sit still thinking about all they had to do to finish getting ready! After church and dinner, the girls took turns making more pot holders and doing the chores around the school. Sarah laughed as she heard Sophie and Emma arguing about where things should go while they were organizing the cupboards in the laundry room. And she had to hide a smile as little Lucy went around carefully dusting the lower tables and every chair, providing some comfort when the little girl inadvertently bumped her head under the table, resulting in a few tears. As she gave Lucy a warm hug, Sarah looked around wondering briefly where Gabbi and Maddi had gotten off to, but Kodi saw her questioning look and quickly told her that the girls had gone upstairs to work on a particularly difficult lesson.

Monday was one of the last days the girls had to work on crafts, so after breakfast, they took turns making pot holders again. They had surpassed the fifty that Sarah had hoped for and, with the loops remaining, hoped to make it to seventy. They were currently working on sixty-one. Olivia and the twins sat near the stack of pot holders, placing each one in a small plastic bag, ready for the craft show. All they had left were the popcorn balls, which were on the schedule for Tuesday. As Sarah packed the hard candy jars in a box for the craft show, she marveled at all they had accomplished in the last few days. Teamwork was amazing, and the support from the adults was more than the girls had ever dreamed of.

Tuesday was a fun day for everyone. The girls spent the morning finishing up the chores they had signed up for and walking around the school showing Miss Maree what they had accomplished. As she checked out the laundry room, she couldn't help but give Sophie and Emma an extra nod of approval. She had heard a bit of the arguing too, but the results of their labor were certainly evident in the neatly arranged shelves and the shining appliances. And when she inspected the bookshelves in the parlor that Sarah had painstakingly dusted and organized, she mentioned that she would like her to accompany her to the bookstore in the near future to purchase some new books for the girls to use. Sarah beamed in response. After Miss Maree had checked off all the chores, she thanked the girls and handed out the money she owed. The girls all thanked her excitedly and hurried upstairs to put the money in their envelopes.

While the girls had been finishing up chores, Miss Jeannie and Miss Jackie had been making popcorn—lots of popcorn! It was spread in big tubs and placed on the table, ready for the marshmallow mixtures that would be colored red and green and poured over the popcorn. As the girls filed into the dining room, Miss Jeannie came in with aprons she and Miss Jackie had made for each of the girls, right down to little Lucy. The aprons had a loop that went over their heads, with ties at the waist that pulled it tight. There were also plastic gloves that the girls could pull on while they were shaping the popcorn balls. As the girls gathered around the table, Miss Jeannie showed them how to put on the aprons and gloves, and passed around a tub of soft butter that they used to coat the gloves so the popcorn and marshmallow mixture wouldn't stick to them while they were forming the balls. Miss Jackie went into the kitchen and brought out the melted marshmallow mixtures. She showed Katie and Kodi how to put a few drops of the colors in and stir them into the mixtures. Soon the girls saw swirls of red and green in the bowls, and the mixtures were ready to pour over the large tubs of popcorn. Miss Maree smiled as the girls took turns reaching into the tubs and grabbing handfuls of popcorn, which soon turned in to red and green popcorn balls.

Miss Jeannie noticed her watching and brought a pair of gloves over to her, showing her how to add butter. "Come on, Miss Maree," she encouraged, "you can make some too!"

Without hesitation, Miss Maree squeezed in between Maddi and Gabbi and reached into one of the tubs to get a gob of the popcorn mixture. Laughing, she worked at shaping the mixture into a ball and proudly added hers to the plate of popcorn balls that was growing quickly. Miss Jeannie and Miss Jackie walked around the table helping where they were needed, adding more butter to gloves and making sure all the popcorn stayed on the table. Once the tubs were empty, Miss Jackie whisked them into the kitchen for cleaning while Miss Jeannie went around collecting the sticky gloves from the girls. Soon all that was left on the table was the large plates of green and red popcorn balls. Sarah tried to count them, and it looked like about forty popcorn balls! She went to the cupboard in the dining room and pulled out more of the plastic bags and ribbons that the girls had cut into small lengths. Using tongs that Miss Jeannie brought out from the kitchen, several of the girls placed each popcorn ball in one of the plastic bags and passed them on to the rest of the girls so they could tie a colored ribbon around the top. They talked and giggled while they were working, with Miss Maree helping the younger girls with the tying, and soon all of the popcorn balls were ready to pack up for the craft show.

"They look so yummy," Nora commented. "I wish we could eat one!"

The girls all agreed enthusiastically, but as Sarah packed the popcorn balls into a box, she reminded them that this was how they were earning money for Santa's Secret Workshop, and eating them would mean less money. The girls nodded, but Miss Maree felt bad about the disappointment she saw on all the little faces. All of a sudden, Miss Jeannie and Miss Jackie came out of the kitchen carrying a large platter of white popcorn balls.

"We didn't color these," Miss Jackie commented, "because these are the *tasting* popcorn balls. We can't sell popcorn balls that we haven't tasted ourselves, now can we? We have to be able to tell customers how good they are, right?"

The excited girls nodded vigorously as Miss Jackie passed around the plate of popcorn balls. Even Miss

Maree got to try one because she had helped. Soon the girls were making comments about how yummy they were, and everyone agreed that they could all tell their customers what a wonderful treat the popcorn balls were. Miss Jeannie and Miss Jackie encouraged the girls to put the ten leftover popcorn balls in bags for the sale, which made fifty popcorn balls in all! As the girls finished their treat and got up to wash hands and get ready for dinner, Miss Maree went into the kitchen to praise Miss Jeannie and Miss Jackie for the successful popcorn-ball production. She was so pleased to have such wonderful ladies working with the girls. She remembered to say a little prayer for all that had transpired since her accident, and once again, she felt the warm glow of God's grace.

20

THE DAY OF THE craft show arrived, cold but sunny. The girls woke up, immediately feeling excited about the coming day. Even Grace stood up in her crib, shaking the side and wanting out to play with the girls. As Sarah lifted her out of the crib, she smiled as she watched her make her way from girl to girl, reaching out for hugs and kisses. She was such a happy girl!

The girls were barely dressed, teeth brushed, hair combed, and beds made when the bell for breakfast rang. The girls hurried downstairs. Today Miss Jackie and Miss Jeannie had laid out fresh cinnamon rolls, milk, and fruit for breakfast. Leaving Miss Maree in charge, they had scurried off to get ready for the craft show. Miss Maree bustled around the girls, pouring milk and breaking up a roll for Grace in her high chair. She seemed as excited as the girls for the craft show! After breakfast, they loaded up the boxes of goodies and piled into the brand-new van that Miss Maree had purchased just for them! It held fifteen passengers, so all the girls could ride together. There was room for Miss Maree, Miss Jackie, and Miss Jeannie too, with a seat to spare for times when they all needed to ride together!

They pulled up to the side door of the church since the craft show was going to be in the basement where the girls had their birthday parties. The older girls all carried a box or bag, and Miss Maree carried Grace and held on to Lucy's hand. When they got inside, the entire basement had been divided into little "squares," with tables on three sides and room to stand in the back. A couple of teenage boys went back out to the van with Miss Jackie to get the rest of the boxes. The girls started unpacking their goodies and laying them out on the tables. Katie and Kodi had made signs for each item, stating the cost, and Sarah was in charge of the cashbox that Miss Maree had lent them. The other girls were encouraged to stand in front of the tables and tell customers all about what they had for sale.

Before long, the girls were attracting a lot of attention! Lucy, Nora, and Olivia were irresistible as they held out different items that were for sale. The pot holders were a hot item, as were the little jars of hard candy, and the girls were kept busy right from the start. Gabbi and Maddi sold all the popcorn balls in the first hour, and Katie and Kodi passed them the last six cookies and moved the rest of the pot holders and candy jars to the front table where they could more easily be seen. Miss Maree took Grace and Lucy and Nora to the ladies' room for a break, but Olivia stayed out front, determined to do her part. Maddi and Gabbi joined her after they sold the last cookie, and they laughed and smiled at customers until the very last jar and pot holder disappeared. The girls were ecstatic and kept asking Sarah how much money they had made. Sarah hushed them with a smile and said they would have to wait until they got home and could count all the money.

Miss Maree suggested they all go over to the tables where the church was providing sandwiches and chips and drinks for all the workers. As they all walked over together, people stopped them and commented to Miss Maree, Miss Jeannie, and Miss Jackie about what a great job they had done and how nice it was to see them all together at church. The adults made sure all the little ones had seats and found a high chair for Grace. Sarah noticed how at ease they had all become and realized they were starting to feel like a real family. Every night, she prayed that things would stay as they were and Miss Maree would not go back to being mean and uncaring. Miss Debbie came over and joined them for lunch and told them all how proud she was of what they had accomplished. She said she would love to come with them to Santa's Secret Workshop on Saturday to help with the little ones so they could all pick out Christmas gifts for one another.

When they finished eating, the tired girls were ready to go home. They hugged Miss Debbie good-bye as Miss

Maree went to get the van, and soon they were on their way back to the school. When they got home, Miss Maree carried Grace upstairs to her crib as the girls gathered in the parlor to find out how much money they had made for Santa's Secret Workshop. Miss Jackie and Miss Jeannie helped Sarah make piles of bills and coins for easier counting. After selling seventy pot holders, sixty snowmen cookies, fifty-five candy jars, and fifty popcorn balls, the girls had a grand total of $290! Since Miss Maree had declared Grace too young to shop for gifts this year, that meant that each of them could have $29 dollars for shopping, in addition to the money they had earned doing chores. It was going to be so much fun at Santa's Secret Workshop!

Saturday could not arrive fast enough for the girls, and Miss Debbie sensed their excitement on Friday when she came for lessons. Since this would be the last school day before the Christmas break, she declared it "game day" for the girls and passed out fun activities that they could do together. There was much laughing and joking as the girls guessed Christmas songs, worked on puzzles, and played charades. Miss Debbie realized how different the school had become for the girls and for her as well. She didn't have to worry about them having enough to eat or wear on a day-to-day basis anymore. Miss Maree seemed to anticipate the things they needed almost before they did, and suddenly the supplies were there without anyone asking. Miss Debbie had noticed the difference in her friend and planned to have a chat with her before she left that day to thank her for everything that she was doing for the girls and the school. As the girls finished their last school activity, Miss Debbie asked them to pack things up for her and went in search of her old friend.

She found Miss Maree downstairs rocking an already sleeping Grace in the big rocking chair that Mr. Frank and his wife had donated to the school. When Miss Maree saw her friend, she stood up and carried the little girl into her bedroom and laid her on the middle of her bed, arranging pillows around her. She invited Miss Debbie to have a seat in her sitting room so they could chat. Miss Debbie smiled at the sleeping Grace and took a seat on the little sofa near her friend's favorite chair.

"How are things going with the girls?" Miss Maree started.

"The girls are doing great," Miss Debbie answered. "It is amazing how much they have grown and thrived in the last year. But I came down to talk about you, Maree. How are you doing?"

"Well, my leg is just about back to normal, and my headaches are gone. I think I am going to be fine, in spite of the accident. It really shook me up, you know."

"Yes, I imagine it did," Miss Debbie replied. "But what about your memory? Did it ever come back? You are so different than you were before the accident."

"Nicer you mean, right?"

"More like the old Maree I knew back in college," Miss Debbie replied. "You have to be aware of the change yourself. I see the way you look at the girls now when you used to completely ignore them!"

"Oh, Debbie, what was I thinking to treat them so badly? Yes, I remember." The tears started in her eyes, and she could not stop them from falling. "I am so ashamed. I was so bitter after losing my second husband I just wanted to die! I thought the school would make me feel better, but it didn't. Then Sarah came along and was so good with the twins, but I resented her too and how much the twins loved her. It just made me a miserable person! And I kept adding more and more girls, trying to make myself feel successful, but nothing helped. It just made me meaner."

Miss Debbie handed Miss Maree a tissue from the table nearby and patted her shoulder. "But you feel differently now, right?"

"Yes, I do," Miss Maree replied. "When I woke up in the hospital and realized how close I had come to death, I was scared. Then Rachel finally found me, and we talked for hours about what had happened, both before and after the accident. At first, I didn't remember everything, but little by little, it all came rushing back. I realized I had always loved the twins, and I almost lost them. They were my last connection to the man I adored, and instead of clinging to them and loving that part of him, I pushed them away. And I remembered Sarah too and knew how badly I had treated her. The way she looked at me when you came to the rehabilitation center the first time cut me like a knife, and I was afraid she would always hate me for the way I had treated her. And baby Grace, just an infant! How could I have been so uncaring?"

"Oh, Sarah isn't like that at all," Miss Debbie exclaimed quickly. "Her parents instilled something very special in her that has only grown over time. She is a very wonderful, caring young lady! And baby Grace adores you!"

"I know, I know," Miss Maree said, "but it still makes me sad to think about how mean and stingy I was with all of them. They have shown me nothing but goodness since I came back home, and I am so thankful to be alive. Sometimes I listen at the top of the stairs when Sarah reads to them from her Bible. That girl is a wonder—the things she has taught them about God and forgiveness and more. It has made me rethink life and my own faith. I didn't even realize how far I had strayed from God until I came back here and heard *her* talking about it! Do you know that in spite of how I treated them all, they pray for me?"

Debbie laughed. "Oh, Maree," she said, "everyone deserves prayers. Don't you remember back in college when we went to that church nearby and the pastor talked about the power of prayer? We were going to change the world by praying for everyone!"

Maree chuckled herself. "Yeah, to be young and invincible again, I can't really remember how that feels."

"Well, maybe you can," Debbie replied. "Give yourself some credit. You have come a long way since your accident. God uses unusual circumstances to reach us at times, and maybe He is using your accident to get your attention and remind you He is there and still has plans for you. All I know is that my friend is back, and I like seeing you enjoy life again. These girls are precious, and so are you, Maree. You all deserve to be happy. Let's start our prayers again and finish our plan to change the world, okay?"

She and Maree both rose to give each other a hug.

"I am definitely with you on that, and I have already started praying again, thanks to Sarah. Now I have something else I would like to talk to you about."

21

THE GIRLS FINISHED PACKING up Miss Debbie's supplies and games and tidied up the upstairs. Sarah noticed that Lucy and Nora were a bit tired, so she offered to stay upstairs with them and read them a story, hoping they would take a little nap. The other girls went downstairs and found Miss Jackie and Miss Jeannie in the kitchen getting ready for dinner, so they offered to help. The ladies put the older girls to work scrubbing vegetables and cutting them up for a salad and snapping green beans to go with their baked chicken and mashed potatoes. Olivia and the twins set the table in preparation for the meal. Miss Jeannie told them to add a plate for Miss Debbie as they thought she might be staying the night since she was going with them to Santa's Secret Workshop the next day. Olivia beamed, happy that Miss Debbie was staying!

Dinner was a happy affair, with the girls all talking about the next day and telling one another what they wanted for Christmas. Maddi was dying to get her ears pierced so she could wear earrings, but Miss Maree told her there was plenty of time for that. "Maybe I will take you on your tenth birthday," Miss Maree continued, smiling, as Maddi looked a little strange.

"Well, I will be ten on January 15, so that is not too far away. I would like that!" Maddi noticed Sarah and Miss Debbie looking at her intently.

"Maddi," Sarah said quietly, "that means your birthday was only a couple of weeks before mine last year. Why didn't you say something when Miss Debbie planned my birthday party? You know I would gladly have shared it with you."

"I know you would have," Maddi said earnestly. "But you worked so hard taking care of all of us, and I didn't want to spoil your surprise. Besides, I enjoyed the party too. It was no big deal. My grandma had lots of parties for me before, and I wanted you to have a special day that was just for you."

Miss Maree walked over to Maddi and gave her a big squeeze. "That was a very selfless thing you did, Maddi, and I am so sorry I didn't mention your birthday to Miss Debbie. You and I will certainly have a little outing this year on your birthday to get those ears pierced, if that is still what you want to do. I am so proud of you, but we will not miss your birthday this year!"

Maddi beamed and squeezed Miss Maree right back. "I love you," she said without hesitation. "You're the best!"

Miss Maree noticed her words and cherished them. Suddenly Miss Jeannie stood up and asked, "Who want's dessert?"

Ten happy girls shouted, "I do, I do," and the eleventh little girl banged on her high chair tray saying: "Me too! Me too!" Everyone laughed as Miss Jackie and Miss Jeannie went to get dessert.

That night, after Gracie was fast asleep and the girls were getting ready for bed, Nora asked Sarah if she would read a story out of her Bible. Sarah smiled and told her she would. The girls all got ready and jumped into their beds in anticipation while Sarah pulled out her Bible and leafed through it, looking for an appropriate verse. Seeing the story about the good Samaritan and his selfless nature seemed like the perfect story for tonight.

"Remember how Miss Maree told Maddi she was proud of her because she was selfless?" Sarah began. "Do all of you know what that means?" When several girls shook their heads no, Sarah continued, "There is a story in my Bible about the good Samaritan," she continued. "It is found in Luke 10:29–37. It's a story about a man who is traveling along a dirt road and comes across someone who has been robbed and beaten and left with no clothes or water or help. This really nice man, the good Samaritan, puts his own plans aside and stops to help the other man. He tends his wounds, takes time to talk to him, and gives him some of his own things, then puts him on his own animal and takes him to an inn so he can get better. He pays for the inn and the man's food and puts his own needs aside. That is really what being selfless is all about."

"I know Maddi wanted to have a birthday last year," Gabbi stated seriously. "But she put that aside so you could have a really special birthday…because you were always giving us your stuff when things were tough. She put her needs aside and made sure you were the one who was taken care of, just like the good Samaritan did. That's why Miss Maree called her selfless, right?"

Suddenly Emma spoke up too, "Well, Sarah, you are selfless too then. You always put our needs ahead of yours."

"That's right," her twin added. "You do do that, Sarah!" Suddenly she realized she had said *doo doo*.

Emma had picked up on it as well. "*Doo doo*? What are you thinking?" Emma hit Sophie with her pillow, which started all the girls laughing.

"Okay," Sarah finally said, "I think you all understand what being selfless is all about. Who wants to pray before we settle down and go to sleep?"

Olivia surprised them all by saying, "I'll pray." The girls all bowed their heads. "Thank You, God, for helping us understand how to be selfless and put others' needs before our own sometimes. We all want to be better girls and be thankful for all we have. Thank You especially for letting Miss Maree get better and not go back to being mean. Help us all to show her how much we like her now, so she will like us back. Thank You for our blessings and for helping us earn money for Santa's Secret Workshop. And thank You for Jesus. Amen."

As all the girls added their own amen, Sarah thought she couldn't have said a better prayer herself!

22

Once again, the girls traveled in the new van to the church the next day for Santa's Secret Workshop. Miss Maree decided to stay home with Gracie since she thought Gracie was still too young to understand the giving and receiving of gifts yet. Miss Debbie offered to drive the van, and Miss Jackie and Miss Jeannie were excited to accompany the girls as well. On the way to the church, Miss Debbie explained that Miss Jill and Miss Becky and Tahler and Destani would be there to help the girls go shopping, along with a girl named Whitney who lived next door to Miss Debbie and went to their church.

When they got to the church, the other ladies were waiting for them. Since there were only nine ladies to the ten girls, Miss Jackie took Lucy, Miss Jeannie took Nora, and Miss Debbie offered to take the twins. Always the social butterfly, Maddi quickly introduced herself to Whitney and grabbed her hand, and Gabbi went with Miss Jill. Miss Becky reached out to Katie, who watched carefully as Kodi paired up with Destani. That left Tahler with Sarah, which was fine with both of them. The big clock at the end of the basement said 10:00 a.m. as all the girls headed in different directions, wanting to find things for one another secretly. Each of the girls had the canvas bag with their name on the front that the ladies at church had made them almost a year ago! They had all agreed to come back in an hour to see how everyone was doing. Miss Maree planned to bring Gracie over to see all the decorations and meet up with the girls at that time.

Sarah had a wonderful time picking out little presents for all the girls. Hair bows and pretty hairbrush sets were only two dollars, and cute rubber animals for the three little ones to use in the tub were even less. A whistle for Maddi to start her songs seemed perfect, and bright red and yellow yo-yos would be fun for the twins. As Sarah's bag got heavier, she wondered what the girls could buy for Miss Maree, Miss Debbie, Miss Jackie, and Miss Jeannie. She talked to Tahler about it, and suddenly they found the perfect gift. She would have to go back and meet up with Miss Maree to borrow Grace for a minute, but she was pretty sure they could make it work if all the girls were willing to pitch in. Tahler was watching the time on her phone, and Sarah had gotten all the girls presents by the time they had to be back. She almost skipped back to the clock!

Miss Maree was already there with Gracie, who was happy to go to Sarah when she walked up to greet them. As soon as the rest of the girls were back, Sarah asked if they could all have a minute to buy one more gift. Tahler offered to go with them, but Sarah made it clear that she didn't want any of the others to come. She noticed the questioning looks as they walked out of sight, but Sarah knew they had to act fast, so she pressed on. She led the girls to a booth and explained what she had in mind. They all smiled and agreed that it was a great idea, and soon they were headed back to the clock with their mission accomplished! The girls all kept their bags up against them, so the others couldn't see what they had purchased. They couldn't wait to get home to wrap their goodies, and they were all excited because Miss Jill and Miss Becky and their granddaughters were coming over for pizza and holiday movies.

When they got home, they piled out of the van just as Miss Jill drove up behind them with Miss Becky and Tahler and Destani. Whitney's mom had picked her up at church, and Maddi was sad to see her go. While they were at the craft show, Miss Maree had set up a wrapping station upstairs, so the girls could go up one by one and wrap their gifts. Miss Debbie and Miss Becky and Miss Jill offered to go upstairs and help the girls wrap. When the last girl had wrapped all her gifts, everyone gathered in the dining room to gobble up the pizzas that Miss Maree had ordered. Afterward, they settled down to watch holiday shows on TV. Sarah was holding Lucy and sat next to Tahler, who was holding Nora on her lap. The two girls smiled as they saw that both the little ones were already half asleep. It was a wonderful day and evening!

The next few days were busy with holiday activities for the girls. Miss Jeannie got out paper and strings and helped the girls make snowflakes to hang in all the windows. They also made pretty Christmas cards to pass out to the elderly at church who might not have families to go to or get cards from.

About a week before Christmas, the doorbell rang, and Mr. Frank stood there holding a big beautiful pine tree. The girls squealed as they realized it was their very own Christmas tree! Mr. Frank set it up in the corner of the parlor and strung endless strings of lights on the tree. Miss Maree brought up boxes of ornaments from the basement that the girls had never seen. As she passed them out to the girls, it seemed like she had a story for each ornament. At one point, Sarah saw her give a hand-painted ornament to Olivia to hang on the tree. There were tears in her eyes as Olivia traced *LAH* on the back, and Sarah realized her daughter must have painted it.

Still, as Christmas music played in the background and the little girls dashed around decorating the tree, it was hard to feel any sadness. The laughter and music filled the room, and happiness seemed to flow out of the woodwork. When the tree was finished and Mr. Frank held Nora high above his head to place the star on top, they all stood back in amazement. It was absolutely beautiful! Maddi grabbed

Mr. Frank's hand and Gabbi's on the other side and started singing "O Christmas Tree." Soon all of them were holding hands, and singing filled the room. Even Miss Jackie and Miss Jeannie were there holding hands with the girls and feeling the spirit of Christmas.

On Christmas Eve, Rachel came over to see the girls and spend the night so she could celebrate with them on Christmas Day. As she came in the door, the girls saw several large bags of presents and watched as she carefully placed them under the tree. As Miss Maree hugged her in welcome, Sarah saw them exchange a bag. Once Rachel had removed her coat and scarf and gloves and hung them in the hall closet, Miss Maree called the girls to gather around the tree, asking them to bring Miss Jeannie and Miss Jackie with them. Once they were all there, she opened the bag and pulled out red velvet stockings with white tops that had each of their names written across the white part. Miss Maree handed out stockings to each of the girls and led them to a small fireplace under the stairway that went upstairs, which the girls had never seen used. Tonight they noticed that someone had decorated it with red garland and sat a little table in front of the grate. Miss Maree showed them little hooks that she had asked Mr. Frank to nail under the railing of the staircase. She told the girls to place a stocking on each hook, starting with Grace at the bottom and ending with Sarah all the way up toward the top. When they were finished, they had a beautiful row of stockings going up the staircase, which Miss Maree said Santa could fill with ease once he came down the fireplace chimney. Before the girls went to bed that night, they helped the little ones place cookies and milk on the little table in front of the fireplace for Santa and a bag of carrots on the shelf underneath it for his reindeer. Sarah thought the girls would never be able to get to sleep that night.

Just before bedtime, Rachel asked the girls if they would like to open an early Christmas present. In seconds, the girls were seated in a circle like little angels, just waiting for her to pass them around. As each of the girls opened their gift, they found warm Christmas pajamas from Rachel. They were supersoft and colorful, and the girls could not wait to put them on. Little Gracie was not going to be left out and had her clothes off and was trying to pull her new pajamas on before they were done opening the packages!

When the girls went upstairs dressed in their pretty Christmas pajamas, Miss Maree insisted on coming with them and tucking them in. Once they were all settled, she pulled up a couple of chairs for her and Rachel and pulled out the Christmas story. As her voice told the story, Sarah thought it was really nice to have someone else read so she could just listen and enjoy it herself for a change.

23

On Christmas day, the girls woke up and jumped out of bed in excitement! Sarah woke up to ten little faces all looking down at her and urging her to get up! Katie had even lifted Gracie out of her crib, and she was sitting next to Sarah, patting her face and saying, "Up, Sarwa, up," Gracie said. Sarah laughed and hugged the little girl.

"Okay, okay!" she said. "I'm getting up!"

The girls brushed their teeth, and Maddi rushed around making sure everyone had their hair brushed, even Katie. They all looked so cute in their new Christmas pajamas that Rachel had given them the night before. It was still too early for breakfast, but the girls were begging Sarah to go downstairs and see if Santa had been there. Sarah was worried about waking up the grown-ups, but they finally persuaded her, promising to tiptoe and not say a word. So Sarah picked up Gracie, and they started slowly making their way down the stairs. As soon as they got down a couple of steps, Gracie started to squeal! Sarah clapped a hand over her mouth as she looked in amazement at the sight before them.

The eleven empty stockings that they had carefully hung up the night before were stuffed with goodies! And under the tree were stacked more presents than any of the girls had ever seen! As Sarah hushed the girls and hurried them back upstairs, she didn't notice the figure standing in the hallway to Miss Maree's bedroom. Miss Maree smiled, feeling the excitement herself and hoping desperately that the girls would be happy about the other surprise she had for them all.

Sarah read the girls stories and encouraged them to make sure they had their own gifts ready to go downstairs. She watched as each of them pulled their gifts out of their hiding places and laid them on their beds, noticing that Katie and Kodi and Maddi and Gabbi were being a bit sneaky about it. The girls were still using the canvas bags with their names on the front. Each girl had her gifts for the others in her bag ready to pass around when they got downstairs. Sarah pulled out her own bag as well, excited to give each of the girls their gift. She walked over to the wardrobe and pulled out the gifts they had gotten for Miss Debbie, Miss Jackie, Miss Jeannie, Miss Maree and Rachel.

At Santa's Secret Workshop, one of the booths had a photographer taking pictures and putting them in frames. The framed pictures were $10 each, but with each of the girls putting in $4, they were able to swing it. Fitting them all in the picture was an even bigger challenge, but the young man taking the pictures had managed to get a *great* picture of all the girls, even managing to get little Gracie to smile her prettiest! Sarah was sure the ladies would love the pictures! The photographer had agreed to throw in an extra photo and frame since they bought so many, so they had one for Rachel too!

All at once, the girls heard the tinkle of the bell announcing breakfast. They hurriedly gathered up their bags and helped Sarah place the photos in a small empty box. They lined up out of habit and followed Sarah and Gracie down the stairs slowly since Gracie insisted on walking by herself. At the bottom of the stairs, all the ladies, including Rachel and Miss Debbie, who had just arrived for breakfast, greeted the girls with warm hugs and holiday greetings. Sarah could not stop smiling as she looked around, although she had a brief moment of sadness remembering last year's pitiful Christmas. She pushed the sad thoughts away, determined to enjoy this year instead.

The girls carefully placed their gifts next to the mountain of gifts around the tree and hurried into the dining room for breakfast. A feast of goodies awaited them, set out buffet style, so even Miss Jackie and Miss Jeannie could enjoy Christmas breakfast with them. The extra table they had used for Thanksgiving was in place, so they could all enjoy the meal together. Fresh fruit, sausage links, mini waffles and doughnuts, and a French toast bake were all arranged down the middle of the tables, with the hottest dishes on the adult table so they could serve them. Soon plates were passed around, and everyone was talking and laughing as they tried to tell one another who wanted what! Gracie, seated in her high chair next to Miss Maree, said, "Me too!" every time someone asked for something. Sarah thought the meal exceeded even the wonderful Thanksgiving dinner they had the month before! She thought she had never seen so many happy faces in her life. It was truly amazing!

The doorbell rang just as they finished breakfast and were beginning to get up to take things into the kitchen. It was Miss Nita and Miss Karen, the two ladies from church who had brought them their winter gear earlier in the month. They brought them a giant red velvet poinsettia and told Miss Jackie and Miss Jeannie they were here to clean up the breakfast dishes and put everything away so they could spend more time with the girls. Everyone laughed as Gracie grabbed Miss Jeannie with one hand and Miss Jackie with the other, leading them into the parlor toward the stockings and presents.

The girls all sat in a circle on the floor, much as they had at Easter, while Miss Maree, Miss Jackie, Miss Jeannie, and Miss Debbie stood up to pass out their Christmas stockings. The girls were surprised at all the goodies that were stuffed inside. They found everything from special Christmas goodies and snacks to practical things like socks, hair ties, and soaps. Each girl had had a special necklace from Miss Jeannie and Miss Jackie wrapped up and tucked in the top of their stockings. In the toe of each stocking, the girls found a wrapped-up popcorn ball. Miss Jeannie and Miss Jackie had saved some extra ones, after all, knowing how much the girls had liked them.

After the stockings were all emptied, the girls took turns passing out the gifts they had gotten each other at Santa's Secret Workshop. Combs and hairbrushes, bracelets, little trinket boxes, and lip glosses were just a few of the items that were unwrapped. When all the girls had exchanged gifts, Miss Debbie nodded to the four older girls. Katie, Kodi, Gabbi, and Maddi stood up while Katie fumbled in her bag. She came out with what looked like a bouquet of shiny papers and ribbons.

Katie stepped toward Sarah shyly and explained, "We wanted you to have something special, Sarah, since you have always taken care of all of us. We know how important your Bible is, so we decided to make you bookmarks for all the stories you have told us over the years. We copied the name of the story and what it meant on pieces of paper and decorated them. Then Miss Debbie took them and laminated them for us. We punched holes in each one to tie the ribbons through. That is why I was using your Bible that day when you came upstairs. Do you like them?"

Sarah stood up to take the bouquet of bookmarks. The first one she looked at had a bright blue ribbon and said "Noah's Ark" on one side. There were funny little animals drawn beneath the title two by two, and on the other side, it said in carefully printed words, "Genesis 6:8: 'But Noah found grace in the eyes of the Lord.'" Sarah looked at all the bookmarks one at a time, till she came to the last one that said, "Amazing Grace." It had a line of eleven little stick figures, with a circle around the littlest one, and the words, "Our gift from God." It had a bright-yellow ribbon, and when she flipped it over, it said, "2 Timothy 2:1: 'You then, my son (or daughter), be strong, in the grace that is in Christ Jesus.'" Sarah was completely overcome, and tears ran unashamedly down her face.

Katie got worried and quickly said, "I didn't hurt your Bible, Sarah, I promise. We were all very careful with it."

Maddi rushed over and hugged Sarah, saying, "We thought you would like to have your special verses on bookmarks, and we all loved your stories so much. Please don't be sad!"

Seeing Sarah's tears, all the girls gathered around her, patting her and telling her they loved her. Noting their concern, she finally managed to say, "You girls are all amazing! I am the luckiest girl in the world! Thank you so much!"

After a few minutes and a few more hugs and reassurances, Sarah convinced them she loved her special bookmarks. Realizing that the other girls were looking at her, she suddenly remembered their presents for Miss Maree, Rachel, Miss Debbie, Miss Jeannie, and Miss Jackie.

As she handed them out, the girls told them they should all wait and open them at the same time. When they opened their packages, all five ladies were surprised. The picture of the girls was so precious, and Sarah saw Miss Maree wipe another tear from her eye as she hugged the picture tight against herself. Miss Debbie and Rachel were beaming, and Miss Jackie and Miss Jeannie just looked at their pictures in awe. The ladies thanked the girls over and over and declared the framed pictures the very best gift of all.

24

It was finally time for the girls to open the rest of the presents under the tree. Each girl got a brand-new book of her own from Miss Debbie, and another new outfit and matching shoes or boots from Miss Maree. She was determined that the girls would never lack for anything again if she could help it. Miss Jackie and Miss Jeannie had gotten all the girls new undergarments, which were desperately needed. When some of the girls blushed upon opening the packages, Miss Jeannie reminded them that it was girls only at the school, so there was no need to be quite so modest. Everyone wore them, after all. Sarah looked around the room at all the new clothes, the happy little girls, and all he wrappings and ribbon and felt so blessed! Gone were the days of trying to make sure all the girls had a clean outfit to wear or begging for the things they needed. Now they each had several brand-new changes of clothing, along with a couple pairs of shoes each. She knew just how lucky they were this year and had reminded the girls to thank the ladies for all the wonderful gifts and the stockings. The girls rushed over to the ladies who had truly changed their lives in the last year and hugged one after another without hesitation. Even Miss Maree felt the love in the room and knew that her school for girls had finally become the success she was looking for.

As the girls scurried around the room picking up wrappings and ribbons, Miss Maree disappeared into her office for a moment. She came out just as the girls finished carrying the last bag of trash into the kitchen and returned to the parlor. Once again, she quietly asked the girls to find a seat. Within moments, eleven pairs of eyes were turned toward her as she stood near the Christmas tree with a paper in her hand.

"I have one more Christmas surprise for all of you that I hope you will like," she started. "And I want each of you to know that you have the right to agree or disagree with what I am about to propose. All of you came here to the school for different reasons, not knowing why or how long you would have to stay." The girls started looking a bit startled, but all the ladies were smiling as Miss Maree went on, "Since you have been here, you have had to deal with some hard times, but I think we have recently become a big family, looking out for one another, taking care of our home and school, and learning how to get along."

Sarah saw several of the girls nod and noticed that Maddi took Gabbi's hand and squeezed it tight.

"I think you would all agree that you have really become *sisters* in the past year, and anyone who watches you take care of one another would think you really are. So I propose that we make it official. How many of you would like to become part of a true family, our family?"

Sarah looked around as all the girls started whispering and looking to Miss Maree for further explanation. "What I mean," Miss Maree finally got out, "is I would like to adopt all of you as my children, forever and ever!"

Complete silence filled the room until Maddi suddenly burst out, "But, Miss Maree, it would cost a *lot* of money to have this many kids!"

Miss Maree just laughed. "Well, money is one thing I do not have to worry about, honey," she said. "I certainly have enough to take care of all of you and the school. These three ladies standing beside me have agreed to be alternate guardians as well, so what do you all say?"

Maddi ran to Miss Maree and hugged her tight. Suddenly everyone started talking and crying and running up to hug all the ladies. When things had finally quieted down a bit, Miss Maree explained that she had discussed this plan with CPS and the few remaining parents or guardians of the girls, with the understanding that they could still visit the school at any time if they wanted to. But the girls would always have a home with her, and she would see to their needs. Miss Maree had gotten approval to legally adopt each of the girls; and Miss Debbie, Miss

Jackie, and Miss Jeannie would have the right to act as their guardians in her absence or if anything happened to her. They would all be one big happy family at last!

"I want you all to think about it," she said. "We will talk about it again on New Year's Eve, and I will need a decision from each of you. Please think about it carefully and write down your answer, no matter what it is. I do not want to move forward with this unless you all are in agreement. Now that is enough! It's Christmas. Let's have some fun!"

Christmas at the Heavenly Home for Girls had surpassed anything Sarah had ever dreamed about. It wasn't just the presents and stockings and food. It was the whole *atmosphere* that filled the house to the very rooftop. It was laughter, and sometimes even tears. It was discovering things about one another and taking care of one another. It was sharing life and knowing you would always have one another's back. It was the knowledge that not one of them would ever be alone again. They could count on one another for comfort and joy, and they could count on the adults in their lives as well. Sarah thought those things were what being a family was really about.

25

New Year's Eve arrived before they had even finished enjoying all their new things. Miss Maree had moved Gracie's crib and changing table downstairs a few days before, so Sarah no longer had the full responsibility of her care. Miss Maree had already adopted Gracie, so she was her little girl now. It was a bit sad for Sarah, but at the same time, it was nice to have more time for her own needs for once. She was almost thirteen now, and Miss Maree had agreed that she would be going to some of the high school classes next year with Miss Debbie. She needed to spend more time on herself, her Bible, and her studies. And she still had nine other girls who looked to her to guide them and show them right from wrong. She took that responsibility seriously, as she had since she was seven years old, and had begun caring for the twins.

Being the first one awake for a change, she looked around at all the sleeping faces and wondered what the future had in store for her and for them. She knew her future was tied to all these girls now, and suddenly she knew who could help her lead them. She got down beside her bed and bowed her head. "Dear God," she prayed, "give me the strength to be who You created me to be. My parents taught me that only You can give me the strength I need to survive and that believing in You will enable me to do even the things that seem impossible. It is that belief that has kept me going without them. It is Your amazing grace that keeps me going today. Be with me as I move forward and give me Your strength in areas where I am weak. Help me to always remember that You know my heart and I belong to You. Thank You for all You have provided us, Lord, and for all You will do in the future. Help me to always remember to be Your servant first. Please give my mom and dad a hug and let them know that they are still loved and never forgotten. Amen."

When the girls awoke that morning, Sarah had come to a decision about Miss Maree. She had written "yes" on a piece of paper and added underneath, "I want to be part of your family." She could hardly wait to give Miss Maree her answer. She hoped all the girls would feel the same, but she would encourage them to write their own answer to Miss Maree. She spoke to the girls after they were all dressed and ready to go downstairs. "I have written my answer to Miss Maree on a piece of paper, folded it in half, and put it in my pocket so it is there when she asks for it. I encourage each of you to do the same. Write your answer on one of the papers I have left on the table and fold it in half so only you have seen it. Please answer on you own and trust your heart to guide you."

The girls all sat down at the table and wrote their answers on the pieces of paper that Sarah had left for them, carefully folding them in half to maintain their privacy. Lucy and Nora told Sarah what they wanted to say, and she helped them get it down on paper. Once it was done, she could almost feel the atmosphere in the room change. They were getting to choose for the first time since they had been at the school, and it felt good. Really good! Now they were ready for Miss Maree, and they could enjoy the rest of the holiday.

The bell tinkled a moment later, and the girls tucked their papers into their pockets and made their way down for breakfast. It was simple today, warm oatmeal with cinnamon and raisins, and crispy buttered English muffins. Gracie was in her high chair at the table and was trying to take her spoon and feed herself. The girls all giggled when she missed her mouth, and the oatmeal ended up above her left eye. Miss Maree smiled, wiping it away and showing her how to put it in her mouth.

Miss Debbie and Rachel arrived after breakfast, planning to spend the last evening of the year with the girls. Miss Jackie and Miss Jeannie would be there too. There were plenty of snacks for later, and it would all be laid out as it had been for Christmas, so everyone could eat what they wanted throughout the evening. This was a new experience for the girls too, and they were both excited and apprehensive about what another year would bring. But first, they had to say good-bye to *this* year. Everyone realized it had been a very challenging year. It had been a year of changes, surprises, and new beginnings; but most of all, it had been a year of growth. The girls had learned so many things—that forgiveness could bring healing, that faith gave you strength, and most of all, that even the hardest person could change if given a chance. They had learned that God's grace was there for *everyone*. All a person had to do was ask.

Everyone played games and worked on puzzles and listened to stories that were read out loud by Miss Debbie, Miss Maree, and even Sarah. The adults and children intermingled, and the adults enjoyed themselves as much as the children did. As early evening approached, they all agreed that watching a movie and staying up to toast the New Year was what they wanted to do. However, before they could all relax and get ready for their first New Year's Eve together, there was one more order of business that had to be taken care of. As Miss Maree stood up, most of the girls knew what was coming.

A ripple of excitement could be felt around the room as Miss Maree began to speak. "I asked you all to think about becoming one family and the possibility of me adopting you. I know it is a bit sudden, but I want you all to know how much it means to me as well. I want to share a couple of things that I hope will help you to understand my actions in the past. And more than anything, I want to ask for your forgiveness.

"I had a little girl of my own once, and I watched her grow up into a beautiful young lady. But I lost her and her daddy because of a car accident. I felt very sad for a long, long time. I thought my life was over. Then a wonderful man came into my life, and I thought maybe I was getting another chance to have a family to love. He had two beautiful little girls who needed a mama, and I loved them all so much." She looked over at Sophie and Emma and smiled.

"But after a short time, my new husband became very ill, and I lost him too. I was sad and angry and bitter. I gave up on everything good in my life and pushed it all away, including my beautiful little girls. When Child Protective Services brought Sarah to me, I took advantage of the situation and used her to care for the girls, never expressing any appreciation for all that she did or what she was going through. I decided to focus on the school for girls I had always wanted, using the name I had come up with long ago. But I didn't do it for the reasons I had back then. I did it only to make money and feel successful. I knew I was being mean and stingy, but I didn't care. The only thing in life that mattered to me anymore was how much money I could make. And I made a lot!

"Then I had my accident, and everything changed. I woke up in pain, and I couldn't remember everything. There was a huge hole in my life, and I didn't know how to close it up. I spent months healing and thinking about what my life had become. And yes, I started remembering…everything. Then I came home, and you were all so kind to me, even though I hadn't treated you well…and I was ashamed. I started paying attention to each of you and saw how special you all are. I saw the things that Sarah had been teaching you, and I was so proud of all that you had become. I want you all to know that I have come to love you, and no matter what the decision about adoption is, you are all welcome to stay at the Heavenly Home for Girls for as long as you want. You are the ones who have made this a heavenly home, and I will never let you down again."

The tears were running down Miss Maree's face as she finished, and Rachel handed her a tissue. The other ladies stood up and hugged her and stayed with her. Finally, she managed a smile and said brightly, "Let's take a vote, shall we?"

One by one, the girls went to Miss Maree and handed her their folded piece of paper. She handed each paper to Rachel as she hugged every girl who came forward, wanting to cry all over again. Finally, Rachel had all the notes and suggested that Miss Maree read them out loud one by one. No one would know who had written the note, but they would all know the answer. Miss Maree opened the first note: "Yes, I want to be part of your family," she read. The girls all clapped their hands. She opened the next note: "Yes, please keep being nice!" There was another round of applause from everyone. The third note simply said "yes!" and once again, everyone clapped. The fourth and fifth notes said, "We want to be your beautiful girls again." There was no doubt about who had written the notes, and the laughter and clapping were plentiful.

The sixth note was very serious. Miss Maree read, "I love you. I want to be part of your family, but please do not ever be mean again. Just pray and God will help you be nice." Miss Maree almost started crying again, and Sarah noticed tears in Olivia's eyes as well. No wonder it had taken her so long to write her note!

"I love you too," Miss Maree said to all of them. "And I promise to ask God to help me be nice."

Notes seven, eight, and nine all said, "Yes"; and as Miss Maree read number ten, it said this: "Yes, I want you to be my mama." The girls suddenly all rose up and ran to Miss Maree, hugging her and laughing.

"We are going to be a real family," Maddi exclaimed. "That means we will all be sisters, even Gracie!" She and Gabbi held hands and danced around in a circle, pulling in Nora and Lucy, who kept shouting, "Sisters! Sisters!"

Sarah walked over to Miss Maree and put her arms around her. She felt like she was hugging a brand-new person, and Miss Maree could not resist kissing the top of her head. They had come so far and overcome so much! And Maree knew now that God had been there the whole time. This young girl, whose parents had taught her to always be faithful, had shown her that God's grace would give her the strength to overcome *all* of life's difficulties. It had opened her eyes and allowed her to see the blessings right in front of her!

Finally, Sarah looked up, and Miss Maree said, "Thank you, Sarah!" As Sarah walked over to Miss Debbie to give her a hug as well, Miss Maree declared, "Congratulations and welcome to the Harper family." She smiled at Rachel, who gave her a thumbs-up! For a second, she thought she saw a shadow at the window, but she blinked, and it was gone. Little Gracie was tugging at her hand, so it was quickly forgotten as everyone snuggled down to watch a movie and welcome in a brand-new year at Mrs. Harper's Heavenly Home for Girls!

EPILOGUE

HE HAD BEEN WATCHING the girls for so long that his fingers and toes were numb. But it was worth it. It was so quiet outside he had even heard most of what they were saying. He trudged back the way he had come, trying to cover his tracks as best he could. It had been almost a year since he left the box on their doorstop, and looking in the window, he knew he had made the right choice. The little girl they called Gracie had to be her. He had made a lot of bad choices in his life, but leaving her there had been a good one. If all those girls were going to be her sisters, she was bound to have a lot of people to take care of her. And she looked well cared for now—and so happy!

As he walked away, he remembered the silent prayer he had left her with. Without thinking, he looked up at the stars in the night sky and said, "Thank you, Lord." He had been staying in an outreach center recently run by a church in a nearby town. Maybe it was time to get more involved and dig deeper into his beliefs. Glancing back at the light shining through the very window he had been standing at, he suddenly found a small ray of hope in his heart. With new determination, he found the old car he had parked on the next street over, climbed in, and headed home.

ORDER INFORMATION

To order additional copies of this book, please visit
www.redemption-press.com.
Also available on Amazon.com and BarnesandNoble.com
Or by calling toll free 1-844-2REDEEM.

CPSIA information can be obtained
at www.ICGtesting.com
Printed in the USA
FFOW05n0634230417
34868FF

9 781683 142560